"Rhiannon, you're definitely a witch," Noah said.

"If I were a witch," she said softly, "I'd find a way to make you kiss me right this minute. I'd put my arms around you like this, and press myself against you like this . . .

Heat wound through his stomach as she slid her arms around his neck.

"Then I'd thread my fingers through your hair so I could pull your head down, and I'd raise my mouth until I could feel your breath on my lips. And then I'd wait . . . and hope . . ."

He crushed his mouth on hers and felt himself begin to fall apart. This was witchery, no doubt about it. Just for a moment, he allowed his need for her to outstrip his need to understand her power over him. He closed his hand around a fistful of golden hair and deepened the kiss. Then he pulled her with him down on the grass. . . .

WHAT ARE *LOVESWEPT* ROMANCES?

They are stories of true romance and touching emotion. We believe those two very important ingredients are constants in our highly sensual and very believable stories in the *LOVESWEPT* line. Our goal is to give you, the reader, stories of consistently high quality that may sometimes make you laugh, sometimes make you cry, but are always fresh and creative and contain many delightful surprises within their pages.

Most romance fans read an enormous number of books. Those they truly love, they keep. Others may be traded with friends and soon forgotten. We hope that each *LOVESWEPT* romance will be a treasure—a "keeper." We will always try to publish

*LOVE STORIES YOU'LL NEVER FORGET
BY AUTHORS YOU'LL ALWAYS REMEMBER*

The Editors

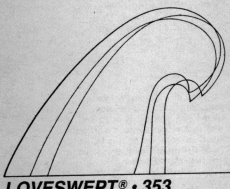

LOVESWEPT® • 353

Fayrene Preston
The Witching Time

BANTAM BOOKS
NEW YORK • TORONTO • LONDON • SYDNEY • AUCKLAND

THE WITCHING TIME
A Bantam Book / September 1989

If you would be interested in receiving protective vinyl
covers for your Loveswept books, please write to this address
for information:

Loveswept
Bantam Books
P.O. Box 985
Hicksville, NY 11802

ISBN 0-553-22023-3

Published simultaneously in the United States and Canada

Bantam Books are published by Bantam Books, a division
of Bantam Doubleday Dell Publishing Group, Inc. Its trademark, consisting of the words "Bantam Books" and the
portrayal of a rooster, is Registered in U.S. Patent and
Trademark Office and in other countries. Marca Registrada.
Bantam Books, 666 Fifth Avenue, New York, New York 10103.

PRINTED IN THE UNITED STATES OF AMERICA

O   0 9 8 7 6 5 4 3 2 1

One

It was a black cat. It was a *very* black cat with a collar of blue crystal beads and a silver bell nestled in the gleaming fur of its breast. And it was sitting on the hood of Noah Braxton's car.

Noah exhaled on a sound of exasperation just as a large pumpkin walked in front of him, bobbed in a semi-bow, and went on.

What next, Noah wondered, and had his question answered as Darth Vader, his dark cloak billowing behind him, made his way across the small park that was located in the center of the town square, and disappeared around the large granite statue of a horse. A mummy strolled nonchalantly on the other side of the old brick street, either unaware or unconcerned that his bandages had unraveled and were trailing along the ground behind him. A dog with a big orange and black ribbon around his neck sat in front of a store window, tilting his head from side to side as if admiring himself.

Noah knew he was in Hilary, Virginia, but he might have driven the yellow brick road into Oz without benefit of signs to warn him of the impending sharp curve that led to unreality.

He'd dictated a tape on the drive down from New York and wanted to send it by express mail to his secretary. He'd expected his stop at the post office to take only five minutes. Instead, he'd found himself expertly grilled by a postmistress with antennae sprouting from her head and who was dressed in a puffy, padded purple costume that made her look like a round bug. He'd been so taken aback by her appearance, she'd been able to extract quite effortlessly every vital fact about his life.

He was thirty-eight years old, had graduated from Harvard Law School with honors, and had a thriving practice, but the things he'd seen in this town in the last thirty minutes amazed him. His gaze returned to the animal on his car hood.

Almost lazily the cat swiveled its head toward him, allowing him to see his pale blue eyes and the glittering sapphire cuff link in his mouth.

Noah stiffened. He'd lost a cuff link just like that one a few weeks ago, but it couldn't be . . . Then he noticed the car window he'd left rolled down when he'd gone into the post office.

The cat stared at him, a calm, aloof, disdainful expression in his eerie blue eyes.

Noah started for him. "You damned cat, give me that cuff link right now."

The cat merely blinked as if to say who, me?

Noah lunged—and grabbed an armful of air. Sprawled across the hood of his car, he turned his head to see the cat sitting on the pavement, gazing up at him with a look that seemed to be as amused as it was taunting.

Straightening off the car, Noah decided to change his tactics. "Here, kitty, kitty."

The cat's eyes took on a you've-got-to-be-kidding gleam. Then, with a flow of sleek muscles and black fur, the cat came to his feet and trotted off across the square, Noah's cuff link still gripped securely in his mouth.

Grim and determined, Noah followed. Black and orange streamers flapped in the late afternoon breeze, the sound blending in a strange way with the whispering rustle of the cornstalks bunched around the electrified gaslights. Jack-o'-lanterns and gourds decorated doorways.

In the center of the little park, beside the statue, the cat stopped and looked back, giving Noah the oddest feeling that the animal was waiting for him to catch up. But by the time Noah reached the statue, the cat was at the edge of the park. And by the time he reached the edge of the park, the cat had crossed the street, having glanced back at Noah one last time before disappearing through the open doorway of a shop in an old Victorian house.

Perplexed, Noah took a moment to study the building. The white wooden house was rather Gothic in feeling, tall, with finials stuck at each pinnacle of the steep roof. All of the windows he could see were raised and had no screens. Cushion, spider, and daisy chrysanthemums in scarlet, white, and yellow filled the flower boxes beneath both the first- and second-story windows.

A sign that said ILLUSIONS hung above the open door.

Long strides took him across the street, through the door of the shop, into another world. Except he wasn't sure if he'd entered a fairy tale or a horror story.

Feather boas and sequined dresses were crammed onto racks side by side with vampire and monster costumes. A shelf ran around three walls of the shop two feet from the ceiling and boasted masks of every description, along with faceless heads that held wigs of varied lengths and bright colors.

Out of the corner of his eye he caught a glimmer of blue. The black cat was enthroned atop a curio cabinet on a blue satin pillow, the cuff link clasped, almost delicately now, between his sharp white teeth.

He had him contained, Noah thought with satisfaction, then let his attention be taken by a shelf of unlabeled jars containing weird-looking sticks and leaves.

This was definitely a creepy place, he decided, and read a sign on one wall that stated UNAT- TENDED CHILDREN WILL BE TURNED INTO TOADS.

Absently he picked up a top hat and found a stuffed rabbit beneath. Unnerved, he reached for a wand but discovered a bouquet of flowers in his hand. A subtle scent of exotic spices and dark flowers drifted to him, invading his senses, and undermining his already slipping grasp on reality.

A young woman walked through a back wall of sheer, iridescent ivory and into the shop. She wore a black high-necked princess-style dress and black high-heeled boots, and her long blond hair fell over her shoulders in wild waves and curls that made her look as if she'd just come in from the wind. Except that outside there was no wind.

Her gaze on the straw broom in her hand, she muttered, "This stupid thing is broken again."

He attempted to clear a sudden obstruction in his throat and wound up making a choking sound.

Her head snapped up. Pale blue, almond-shaped eyes transfixed him. He'd never seen eyes quite like hers before. They slanted downward, giving them a mysterious, beguiling appearance. But it was their enigmatic blue depths that mesmer- ized. And, he realized, they were the exact shade, with the same hypnotic potential, as the cat's.

"May I help you?"

Her voice was like a piece of velvet shaped into low, soft, melodic notes, he thought, bemused, bothered.

When he said nothing, she tilted her head to one side. "If you just want to stand there, I can let you have the spot rent-free for a week. After that, though, I'm afraid I'll have to charge you."

The unexplainable bizarre atmosphere of the town and the otherworldly feeling of the shop had worked on his mind. And then there was her windblown hair. He had to ask. "What's wrong with your broom? Too much mileage?"

Her brows rose ever so slightly, her whole demeanor cool and regal. Again he was reminded of the cat.

"Who are you?" he asked hoarsely.

"Rhiannon," she said. "Rhiannon York."

"Wasn't Rhiannon a Welsh witch?"

"Legend and history sometimes do a person a terrible disservice. Personally I've always felt Rhiannon was a greatly misunderstood person."

The ground gently shifted beneath him. "What is this place?"

"Illusions. It's a costume and magic shop. What did you think it was?"

"I wasn't sure."

"Would you like to rent or buy a costume?"

Her voice was like a soft caress, putting him under a spell. "No. I want my cuff link back."

She studied him, and he had the odd, uncomfortable feeling she found him amusing. "What makes you think I have a cuff link of yours?"

"I don't think, I *know*. Your cat stole it."

Her gaze went directly to the cat atop the curio

cabinet as if she'd known he was there all along. Noah looked too. Amazingly a seraphic expression graced the cat's face. And there was no sign of the cuff link.

"He had it," Noah said. "I tell you, I saw it in his mouth."

"Of course," she said gently. "Can you describe the link?"

His teeth came together with a snap. "It's a square sapphire in a gold setting."

She pushed the top hat and stuffed rabbit aside and laid the broom on the counter. "Graymalkin, come to me."

With boneless fluidity and a crystal tinkling of the silver bell around his neck, the cat flew from the top of the cabinet and into her arms.

"What have you been up to, Graymalkin?" she asked scoldingly yet soothingly. "Have you been naughty?"

The cat closed his eyes and purred with contentment.

The sight greatly irritated Noah. "Why does a black cat have a gray name?"

"I named him after the cat in *Macbeth*."

He made the connection immediately. Graymalkin was the name of Witch One's familiar. Then he remembered how *this* particular cat had literally led him here to her. "Does your cat do errands for you?"

The corners of her mouth turned upward in a way that completely beguiled him.

"Only very special errands, Mr. Braxton."

He went still. "You know who I am?"

"If you're Noah Braxton, I do."

"That's impossible. I've been in this town exactly forty-five minutes. No one knows my name." A sudden picture of the postmistress flashed into his mind. "No one, that is, except a smiling purple bug."

"Oh, you met Edwina."

Nothing was making sense. "What in the hell is going on in this town anyway? Why all the decorations and costumes?"

"Halloween, Mr. Braxton. All Hallow's Eve."

"Halloween?" He frowned and quickly computed the date. "But this is Thursday evening. Halloween isn't until Monday evening."

"Halloween is a tradition in this town. Everyone goes all out, and we believe in starting early with our celebration."

"But why Halloween? I mean, why not the Fourth of July? Thanksgiving?"

"Everyone in town decided long ago that it's much too hot on the Fourth to be able to throw ourselves into that holiday with any sort of real enjoyment at all. Thanksgiving . . ." She shrugged. "Besides, there's the legend."

He stared at her, feeling as if he were being pulled into the hypnotic blue depths of her eyes. "You got me off the subject," he said, surprised to hear his words come out in a raspy whisper.

"What was the subject?"

"I want to know how you know my name." He felt a small sense of relief that he'd been able to force his voice to return to normal.

"Your aunts, Esme and Lavinia DeWitt—they're very good friends of mine and my grandmother's, and they told me you were coming to visit them this weekend."

Niggling doubt remained. "But why did you think *I* was their nephew?"

She gave him a sweet smile that made him feel as though he might dissolve. But her next words made him stiffen his spine.

"They described you. They said you were very nice, but, unfortunately, very uptight."

The muscles in his jaw constricted. "The *other* subject you nearly made me forget was my cuff link. Where is it?"

"I haven't the slightest idea, but I'll be glad to help you look." She opened her arms and Graymalkin leapt to the floor and disappeared through the back wall.

Noah looked hard and saw that a long length of sheer, shiny fabric curtained off a back room from the shop. He was comforted by the logical explanation, but, he decided, the sooner he got away from this strange place, the better off he'd be.

He felt as if his mind was bending so that he saw things that weren't there, imagined things that couldn't be. He glanced at the broom on the counter. Now he could see that the handle had come away from the straw bottom. It made sense.

But there was still *her* to explain—this extraordinary woman with the deep, enigmatic blue eyes.

"I'll check around Graymalkin's pillow," she said, "and you search anywhere else you like."

He stood, staring after her as she threaded her way through the racks of costumes and display cabinets. No one—man or woman—had ever left him feeling so completely disconcerted.

"How did Graymalkin get your cuff link anyway?" she asked, standing on tiptoe on a stepstool and running her hand over and under the blue satin pillow the cat had been sitting on.

With her arms raised, he was offered an enticing side view of her high, full breasts.

An inquiring glance over her shoulder prodded him to answer her question. "He must have gone in through the open window of my car while I was in the post office."

"You keep your cuff links in your car?"

"I lost this link a week or two ago. I wasn't sure where. Fortunately I keep extras at the office."

"Prepared for any contingency," she said without emphasis, and climbed off the stepstool.

"I wasn't prepared for this," he muttered under his breath.

Somehow she heard.

"I know it must be distressing to lose something you regard so highly, but you really should guard those things that mean so much to you."

He realized she was talking to him in the same scolding yet soothing tone of voice she'd used with Graymalkin. He'd never been talked to like a cat before.

"In the first place, it wasn't my fault that I lost the link. The tension on the post must have been weak so that it slipped out of my shirt sleeve without my being aware of it. In the second place, I feel no sentimental attachment to the damned thing. It's just a very expensive cuff link that I wear occasionally."

"Of course. I understand completely." She peered behind the curio cabinet, then bent to search the floor. "It's not here. Have you had any luck?" She straightened and regarded him expectantly.

He hadn't even looked, he thought, and she knew it. Those slanted eyes of hers were not only mysterious but dangerous. He should break eye contact, but the floral, spicy scent that had been with him ever since he'd entered the shop had gone to his head, making it difficult for him to think. It was a rich, pervasive fragrance that held a promise of enchantment. "What is that smell?"

She crossed to a small table by him that held an assortment of candles, all sizes and shapes. "It must be the scented candles."

The scrap of a match against flint sounded loud to his ears, and the flame she held to the candle's wick until it lit seemed inordinately bright. "Aren't witches afraid of fire?"

She blew out the flame with a soft puff of breath. "You must be thinking of the times when sus-pected witches were burned at the stake."

He blinked, unsure why he'd asked such a stupid question. He *never* asked stupid questions. And the last witch that had occupied his thoughts for any time at all had been the one in "Hansel and Gretel," when his mother read him the story at age four.

Her smile held a knowledge he couldn't comprehend.

"Fire is an element," she said, "and one of the supposed powers of a witch is the ability to control the elements."

Damn. Why did she bother him so? He reached out and pulled her to him. "It's not the candles I'm smelling," he said gruffly. "It's you."

"But I don't wear any perfume."

"It figures." He had a firm grip on her arm, yet he felt as if she were tugging at him, drawing him toward her. He wanted badly to kiss her. Ludicrous. He didn't even know her.

"Do you find the scent unpleasant?"

"I find it drugging. And you, blindingly beautiful. You're a witch, aren't you?"

She raised her free hand and gently caressed his lean jaw. "You must be tired. You've had a long trip today."

"Yes, I have."

With a simple movement she broke free of him. "You should go on out to Esme and Lavinia's. They're waiting for you with a good supper and a soft bed."

"Soft bed," he repeated, in a trance and unable

to look away from her. _Her_ and a soft bed. He wanted to make love to her. His body received the thought with a jolt of heat.

"I'll find your cuff link. Leave now."

Step by slow step he walked backward out the door, keeping her in his sight. Gradually the distance between them and the dimness of the shop intervened until all he was able to see was her slender silhouette and the pale gold nimbus around her hair, a reflection from the candle.

Out on the sidewalk he felt his gaze drawn upward.

Graymalkin sat in the upstairs window, staring down at him with his eerie, enigmatic blue eyes.

Noah glanced back into the shop. Rhiannon was no longer there.

Lavinia DeWitt's lavender hair resembled an exotically colored bird's nest, Noah decided fondly, watching her absently pat at it.

"We're so glad you've come to visit us, Noah," she said. "It's been too long since we've seen you."

Her sister, Esme, nodded in agreement while passing him the ham. "It was a real treat, taking the train to New York City to see you like we did for all those years, but it's become so hard—"

He managed to take the serving plate from Esme only a second before the ham would have slid off, down through the white vaporous fog that hovered over the table, and onto the bright orange tablecloth. He looked again at the dry-ice-induced fog, billowing out of the jack-o'-lantern centerpiece. His aunts seemed so pleased with the effect, he hated to mention that the food was getting cold. He helped himself to a thick slice of country ham, then set the platter aside.

"—for us to travel," Lavinia said, picking up where Esme left off. "My arthritis, you know. But, my goodness, we've certainly missed you. You're our only link to Rebecca now that she's gone."

His mother, Rebecca, was their younger sister and had died two years before. At the mention of her name, Noah felt a gentle tug of loss. His mother had been a saner, more sophisticated version of Esme and Lavinia, loved and adored by her Wall-Street-broker husband and her son.

"You're our only living relative," Esme added.

Esme's hair color ranged somewhere between pink and strawberry, depending on which section of her hair you looked at. Oddly enough, Noah thought, his aunts had always seemed to him exactly as they did at this moment. Each year had added only a few more wrinkles.

"I should have come before," he acknowledged with complete sincerity. "I've missed you, too, but my law practice keeps me working eighteen hours a day." Esme bestowed an understanding smile on him that made him feel worse than he already did at having waited so long to visit his aunts.

"Young people lead such busy lives these days," she said. "Have some iced tea, dear."

"I'll pour it," he said, quickly reaching for the heavy-looking pitcher.

"Did you know that your mother was born in this house?"

"Yes, Aunt Lavinia." He threw a surreptitious glance at the faded and peeling wallpaper and decided his mother had probably sat at this same table as a little girl and looked at those same flowers. He knew for a fact that his aunts were financially secure, but they obviously didn't go in for a lot of decorating. Except for Halloween.

"Well, it's only right and proper that you're here now," Lavinia said. "This house and this town were your mother's home, and you should get to know them."

"And it's such a perfect time for you to be here," Esme said, her wrinkled cheeks plumping as she beamed at him. "There's the Halloween celebration, and everyone expects the legend to happen this year."

He looked up. Rhiannon had mentioned a legend.

"Rhiannon says the roses have never looked more beautiful," Lavinia said.

His pulse accelerated at the mention of the woman he hadn't been able to get out of his mind. He put down his fork and rested his forearms on the edge of the table. "I met Rhiannon in town earlier."

Lavinia brought her hands together in delight. "How *nice* that you've already met. She's such a lovely girl. We think—"

"—the world of her," Esme interrupted to finish Lavinia's sentence.

"She's . . . a little spooky," he said, and immediately grimaced. He was a logical, intelligent man, with a good education, a successful career, and something of a reputation for eloquence. But for some reason he couldn't articulate his confused feelings. It was almost as if Rhiannon had bewitched him.

Esme waved her hand back and forth through the white mist until she could locate the bowl of sweet potatoes. She helped herself to them. "Spooky, dear? Did she have on a ghost costume?"

"No. She was dressed all in black, as black as her cat. Have you ever noticed that her cat's eyes are the same color as hers?"

Lavinia happily nodded her agreement. "It's a wonderful shade of blue, isn't it? I've always loved it."

"But the cat . . . he's strange, don't you think?"

"You're just not use to cats, dear," Lavinia said.

"Since your mother was allergic to them," Esme said.

Unconsciously he folded one hand into a fist. "I know I've never been around cats much, but I still think there's something very weird about him. Did you know that she named him after the cat in *Macbeth*?"

"Now that you mention it, he does look rather Shakespearean with that little pointed chin and those adorable whiskers."

Lavinia smiled. "And there is something kingly about him."

"The cat in *Macbeth* wasn't a king," he said, striving to be patient. "He was a familiar, and this cat actually *led* me to Rhiannon."

"That was very thoughtful of him, and convenient for us. We were going to introduce you to Rhiannon, but now we won't have to." Lavinia looked to her sister for confirmation that she was equally pleased.

Esme's smile said she was. "Graymalkin is the dearest thing. We take him little goodies from time to time."

"We have to go to him," Lavinia said. "He never comes this far out of town."

Noah sighed. His aunts were very sweet and unfortunately quite batty. He should put Rhiannon and her cat out of his mind and remember why he had come to Virginia. He was in his element solving problems, and it seemed his aunts might have one.

"About the letter you sent me, Aunt Esme and Aunt Lavinia. You wrote that you'd had an offer to buy this land and at a very good price. Now, you didn't come out and say it, but I sensed that for some reason you were uneasy."

The two ladies exchanged glances. Esme looked down at the napkin in her lap. "We don't want to sell, Noah. This land has been in our family for generations. When we die, you'll inherit."

He shook his head with impatience. "My inheriting shouldn't enter into your decision. But I can understand why you wouldn't want to sell. What I don't understand is why you feel uneasy. What's the problem?"

Esme and Lavinia once more exchanged a glance. Lavinia was the one who spoke this time. "It's just that the offer is way over the actual value of the land."

He smiled. "I can't think of many people who would see that as a problem."

"Yes, well, a couple of things have occurred that make us—"

"—wonder."

Noah sat back in his chair. "Okay, tell me."

"Three other landowners, all of whom live on this side of town, were sent the same letter, offering the same high amount of money for their land," Esme said. "They didn't want to sell, either, but in the end they did."

He shrugged. "So they changed their minds."

Lavinia gave an unladylike snort. "They certainly did change their minds, and that's not all. Justin McMurphy, one of the landowners, swore off drink when late one night he saw a Yankee soldier riding across his field, brandishing a bloody saber."

Noah frowned. "Had the man been drinking?"

"Oh, there's no doubt about that."

"Justin drank like a fish," Esme said, "and did for years. The point is, we've never had a Yankee soldier ride anywhere other than the town's main street. And naturally that's a special case."

"Esme's right. Of course, the boy's never been known for his punctuality, but this is much too early even for John Miller."

"Who are we talking about?" Noah asked, suddenly confused.

"John Miller, dear. Then there was Elizabeth Dailey. Never known her to be skittish, but all of a sudden she upped and went off to live with her daughter in Richmond. Said she was hearing too many strange noises."

"And what about Fred Willingham?" Lavinia asked her sister. "A county health official came out to his place not too long ago, said he was making routine random checks of the wells in the area. Made his check, then told Fred he had a high concentration of lead everywhere and the water wasn't fit to drink. Fred and his family were hit hard by the news. Not two hours later, a truck came out bringing them bottled water for drinking. Mighty nice of someone, but the bottom line was Fred panicked. He didn't even have the sense to get a second opinion."

"Or even to check out that county health official. Fred just agreed to sell, took the upfront money, and left."

Noah looked from one to the other of his aunts. "So three people have recently moved off their land and agreed to sell because of something odd." He paused. "Has anything strange or unusual happened here?"

"No," Esme said. "And we may be letting our

imaginations run away with us. Our friend Gladys York has land on this side of town, too, and nothing unusual's happened to her."

"Of course she hasn't been here this last week for anything to happen. Rhiannon sent Gladys—"

"Gladys is Rhiannon's grandmother," Esme said, seeing the puzzled look on Noah's face.

"—on a month-long visit to her sister in Wales."

"Gladys's birthday isn't until next month, but Rhiannon decided to give her grandmother the trip as an early present. Wasn't that nice of her?"

He wasn't sure whether Rhiannon was normal enough to have a nice motive or not. His life was grounded in reality, but less than a day in this town had shown him these people didn't know the meaning of reality. And that included his aunts. The events they described could be chalked up to coincidence or even to flights of fancy. He'd feel much better about going back to New York and leaving his aunts out on this farm by themselves if he found reasonable explanations for these events.

"Who's making the offers?"

"No one knows. The letters are being sent by a lawyer in town—"

"—named Clifford Montgomery."

"But he says he's acting for a client he claims has asked that his name be kept confidential for the time being." Lavinia looked disgusted. "Can you imagine? He wouldn't even tell *us*."

"Even when we promised not to tell anyone."

Noah came to a decision. "I've made arrangements to stay until Sunday morning. That gives me two days here. I'll check around and see what I can find out."

"Two days," Lavinia said. "We were really hoping you'd stay longer."

Esme turned to her sister, a determined brightness fixed on her face. "Still, Lavinia, a lot can happen in two days."

Lavinia nodded at her sister, and a communication passed between the two. "Yes, I suppose you're right."

They both smiled beautifully at Noah.

"Are you ready for some apple cobbler now, dear?"

Noah lay, staring up at the ceiling, in the bed his mother had slept in as a child. The autumn night breeze filtered through the openwork of the lace curtains and fanned across his tired body.

Images of the beguiling, mysterious Rhiannon played through his thoughts, keeping him awake. She'd clouded his mind with her spellbinding ways and woven a web of sensuality around him. For a wild, incredible flash of time, he'd actually wondered if she was a witch.

The explanation was obvious. He'd been working too hard.

He'd get a good night's sleep, visit with his aunts, find out what, if anything, was going on with the land, and leave in two days. There would be no reason for him to see Rhiannon again. He shifted to a more comfortable position, pleased with his plans.

The wind blew. He heard a soft, tinkling sound. The curtain fluttered and shifted aside. He glanced toward the window.

A black cat wearing a collar of blue crystal beads and a silver bell sat on the windowsill, gazing at him through the darkness. The cat was so still, he appeared to be a statue. Then he turned his head just enough so that his eyes caught the moonlight and flashed like blue neon.

Back in town, curled up on her bedroom window seat, Rhiannon stared out at the night and smiled.

Two

Rhiannon leaned out of the upstairs window and gazed down on the top of Noah's head. She felt immensely satisfied. He was glowering at the front door of her shop and hadn't realized yet that she was above him. She decided to wait a minute before announcing her presence. With a man like Noah Braxton, it was best to take what advantages you could.

Lavinia and Esme had talked about him for years, but she'd put their bragging down to the bias of two loving, doting aunts who'd never had children of their own. They'd told her he was handsome, but they hadn't described the deep brown shade of his eyes and the intense way he had of looking at a person. And they hadn't told her about the short, controlled style of his rich brown hair that made her want to run her fingers through it and mess it up. They also had failed to relate the elegant way clothes dressed his tall, lean frame.

It hadn't taken her long at all to know that he was an intelligent, too serious, extremely virile man. And she wanted him.

She'd never been drawn so strongly to a man before, but the suddenness and complete certainty of the attraction hadn't taken her aback. She'd been born with a gift for knowing what was right for her, and she rarely looked beyond her own instincts for help in making a decision. She'd thought about him all night, and if sheer will could summon a person, it had.

With stiff impatience he raised his hand and rapped his knuckles hard against the door. It was the fourth time he'd knocked, she calculated.

"Good morning," she called.

He tilted his head back, glanced up, and caught his breath. Rhiannon looked as if she'd just gotten out of bed . . . or just come in from an all-night ride among the stars. And he couldn't decide which idea was more intriguing.

Her golden hair fell over one bare, ivory-hued shoulder and down to the beginning swell of her breasts. The windowsill hid the rest of her from him, but his imagination drew a picture that made his mouth go dry.

"I don't usually open the shop this early," she said, "but if there is something you saw yesterday that you want . . ."

The answer that sprang readily to his lips was instantly suppressed as his legal training came to his rescue. "I'd like to talk to you, but I'll wait while you dress."

"I won't be a minute," she said, and disappeared into her room.

Noah slipped his hands into the pockets of his slacks and glanced around. Other than a scarecrow walking his dog, there didn't seem to be anyone about.

He supposed he was early, but sometime during the night he'd changed his mind about not seeing Rhiannon again. It had occurred to him that she could have some information that might help him. Among other things, he wanted to know whether it had indeed been simply a nice gesture on her part to send her grandmother to Wales for her birthday or if she'd had another reason for doing so.

His gaze drifted to a thicket of wild roses that grew on a small patch of land to the side of Rhiannon's house, then continued on to the center of the park, where the imposing statue of the horse stood, its gray granite head up, its eyes alert, a bridle around its neck. There was something odd about that statue. . . .

The door opened behind him and he turned to see Rhiannon, incredibly beautiful in a black silk kimono-style robe. The rush of heat through his body forced him to admit that there'd been another, more compelling reason that he'd come so early. An urgent, almost desperate need to see her again had brought him to her—and, despite his rationalizations, very little else.

"Come in," she said softly, and backed away so that he could enter the shop. "Do you feel better this morning?"

"Better?" The gleaming black silk gave her skin a seductive luminosity that made his fingers tingle with a desire to touch.

She shut the door behind him. "You seemed so tired yesterday. Were you able to get a good night's rest?"

"Yes, although I didn't fall asleep as soon as I thought I would. I had a visitor."

"Oh?"

"Your cat decided to pay me a visit."

She smiled gently. "Graymalkin loves to wander at night."

Her smile made her face even more beautiful, but forces were at work he didn't understand, and he couldn't let the matter alone. "My aunts mentioned earlier in the evening that he never comes out as far as their farm."

"That is a little far for him to go," she admitted. "By the way, I still haven't found your cuff link."

He looked at her blankly. There had to be a reasonable explanation. Didn't there? "Where is Graymalkin now?"

"I haven't seen him this morning," she said, her tone serene and unconcerned. "He comes and goes at will. He's very much his own person."

"You mean *cat*, don't you?" He didn't need the odd look she shot at him to make him regret what he'd said. His imagination was working overtime, creating nerves he hadn't known he had. But then, before he came to Hilary, Virginia, he hadn't been aware he had an imagination.

She led the way through the shop, moving as a ballerina danced—graceful and fluid, almost as if her feet didn't touch the floor. Was she real, he wondered. Was it possible that she could control the elements? More important, did he have a snow-ball's chance in hell of keeping her from control-ling him?

Without warning, something heavy and oppres-sive enclosed him, tangling around him. It cov-ered his face so that he couldn't see or breathe. He hit out at it, trying to free himself, but it wrapped more tightly around him, suffocating him. Then he heard the soft velvet tone of Rhiannon's voice.

"Noah? Noah, what are you doing?"

His heart beating wildly, he waited, willing the return of calm and control. After a few moments he took several backward steps until he could see that he'd walked into a rack of costumes. He'd been fighting the cloak of the Phantom of the Opera, and he felt like a complete and utter fool. "I guess I wasn't watching where I was going."

Her smile held sympathy. "The shop is terribly crowded, isn't it? Just follow me, and you won't get lost."

Following her was how he'd gotten into the predicament in the first place, he thought. But maybe it didn't matter. Maybe he was already lost.

She disappeared through the sheer iridescent curtain. He hurried after her and discovered himself in a back room that was as packed with costumes, masks, and assorted props as the main part of the shop. "What do you do with all this stuff after Halloween?" he asked curiously.

"This isn't a one-season business. During Thanksgiving, pilgrim costumes are in big demand, and around Christmastime, Edwardian costumes come into vogue. Theater groups from four states call me for costumes all year long. And then there are the magicians that come in to stock up on the supplies of their trade."

He gave a short laugh. "I think I ran into some of your magic yesterday. There was a rabbit in a hat and a wand that turned into a bouquet of flowers."

She grinned. "I keep them there for the children. They get a kick out of them."

"I did too," he said dryly, remembering how unnerved he'd been by the town and the shop and then by her.

Logical explanations—everything and everyone had them. He hung on to the thought.

They climbed a wooden stairway to one large room that took up the entire second floor. It wasn't too strange that she lived in one big room, he told himself. A couple of his friends in New York lived in lofts.

And it seemed to be decorated normally, he decided, relieved. The room was furnished with dark wood antiques that were upholstered and pillowed in materials of a deep royal purple color, patterned with orchid, mauve, and wine flowers. The darkness of the room was lightened by windows on four walls, along with lengths of the now-familiar sheer iridescent ivory fabric draping the walls and the big bed.

The bed. He did a double take. The bed was a swing suspended from the ceiling by four thick brass chains.

He turned to her, a question on the tip of his tongue, and froze. A small owl was sitting on her shoulder.

"This is Merlin," she said as if she were introducing him to a friend.

"How did he get on your shoulder?"

She laughed at the intensity of his question. "He flew, of course. The movement of an owl's wings is nearly silent."

"But . . . what's he doing here, in your house."

"He lives here with Graymalkin and me. I found him when he was just a few days old, huddled on the ground by my grandmother's barn. I searched, but there was no sign of his mother or even a nest."

"Didn't that seem a little odd to you?"

Her eyes twinkled. "You are from the city, aren't you? Unfortunately similar things happen all too frequently. Besides, I didn't really think about it.

He was a small, helpless creature who needed caring for, and I did it."

She turned her head, and bird and woman exchanged a long look. Then the owl touched his beak to her cheek in what looked for all the world to Noah like a kiss.

"Fly away, Merlin," she said softly. The bird lifted its wings, took flight, and seconds later landed on top of an armoire in the bedroom area.

He couldn't let the matter pass. "Rhiannon was supposed to have three magical birds who could lull the living to death, wake the dead to life, and heal all sadness and pain."

She tilted her head to one side and regarded him thoughtfully. "Yes, I believe you're right. Have a seat, Noah. I'll pour us some coffee."

Okay, he told himself, so she had a bird and a cat. A lot of people had birds and cats for pets. Noah sank onto the nearest sofa. "What does Graymalkin think of Merlin?"

"They get along beautifully," she said in the little kitchen area, setting the sugar bowl and the creamer onto the tray along with two cups of coffee.

A funny sensation skidded along his spine. Birds and cats were natural enemies. "How do you explain that?"

As she walked across the room to him, the lower portion of the robe parted, giving him a glimpse of long, shapely legs. She placed the tray on top of an old trunk that served as a table and came down beside him. "Do you need an explanation for everything?"

"Yes, I do. And preferably one that makes sense."

She leveled an amused gaze at him. "Esme and Lavinia were right. You're very tightly wound. You need to relax, take things a little less seriously." Suddenly she reached out and stroked her hand along the side of his face. "You shaved this morning, didn't you? Your skin feels wonderful. But then, I liked the raspiness of your five-o'clock shadow yesterday afternoon."

"Rhiannon—"

She held up a finger. "Don't ask me why I just touched you. Figure it out for yourself. Then next time you'll know whether you want me to touch you or not."

Fire ignited in the pit of his stomach. There was no question that he wanted her to touch him again. And again. *No.* He brought himself to a screeching mental halt, refusing to allow his thought processes to progress any further. He had to concentrate on something else, something real and solid. Like a problem. "I've come here this morning for a reason, Rhiannon."

A jewellike flame flickered and flared deep in her eyes, fascinating him.

"Whatever the reason, I'm glad you're here."

She *was* a witch, he thought. What other explanation could there be for his brain turning to mush?

"Drink your coffee," she said.

He didn't have to be coaxed. He dumped three spoonfuls of sugar and several dollops of cream into the cup and drank it down. Afterward, he felt much more in control, but just to be safe, he got up and moved a few feet away from her. "My aunts tell me that your grandmother lives east of town, out by them."

It seemed to him that a subtle change came over her, and her smooth brow creased with concern.

"Yes. Her land adjoins theirs."

"They also told me about the high offers for the land in that area and the things that have occurred to convince three of the owners to sell."

"Yes. There have been some strange things happening, and I'm not sure what to make of it all."

He felt better. She actually considered something strange. And her uncertainty made her seem human. He massaged his eyelids with his thumb and finger. *Of course she was human.* "Has your grandmother received an offer?"

She nodded.

"And you sent her to Wales because of it."

"I wanted her away from here until I could look into the matter. Unfortunately the Halloween rush has kept me from doing anything yet."

Forgetting his need to keep a distance from her, he took up the place beside her he'd vacated only seconds before. "Well, I have the time, and I plan to discover what's behind these offers before I leave town on Sunday. I was hoping that you might be able to tell me something that would help. Have you lived in this town your entire life?"

"No. My father was in the service when I was growing up, and we lived all over the world. The moves were a constant upheaval. But I spent every summer here with my grandmother, and after I got out of school and did some traveling on my own, I decided to settle here."

The father she'd mentioned had caught his attention. "Is your father still in the service?"

"No, he's retired. He and mother live in Washington, D.C., and he works in the Pentagon."

She had parents. Did witches have parents? Of course they did. But surely the Pentagon wouldn't allow a parent of a witch to . . . He almost groaned aloud. *He had to stop this.* "So when you came back here to stay, you bought this shop?"

"I bought this house and made it into the kind of place I wanted it to be. I've been here seven years now."

Intrigued, Noah thought over what she'd just said. She was a woman whose unusual beauty could make her a fortune in any capital of the world. She'd traveled extensively, and he was willing to bet that everywhere she'd gone, men had tried to make her theirs. Yet in the end she'd chosen to live in this small, out-of-the-way town. Her self-confidence told him she knew what she wanted. Her serenity told him she was happy with her choice. But he didn't understand. "What do you *do* here?"

She smiled. "I do exactly what I want. I spend a great deal of time with my grandmother, I run my shop, I see my friends, I do volunteer work at the hospital. There's no end of things to do if you're interested in life."

At this moment her eyes were completely clear. He could detect no guile or deception. Yet she remained a mystery to him. "I've gotten off track," he muttered, more to himself than to her. "I was really trying to find out how well you knew the town and its people."

"Very well. But I have no idea what's going on." Suddenly she reached out and touched his arm. "I'm driving to my grandmother's this morning to check on things. Why don't you come with me? You arrived at your aunts' place late yesterday, and you haven't had a chance to see much. Maybe, between us, we can figure out why someone would want the land."

He looked down. He'd rolled his shirt sleeves back this morning so that his forearms were bare. In the act of removing her hand, she slid her fingers lightly across his skin, leaving a searing trail.

"Well?" she asked softly.

"I think that's a good idea."

"Then I'll get dressed." He started to get up, but she stopped him. "Stay where you are. It won't take me long." She walked to the tall armoire, opened the doors, and chose a pair of black jeans and a black sweater. Then she disappeared behind a lacquered screen.

Noah was left gazing into the open armoire. Every article of clothing in it was *black*.

From atop the antique wardrobe, the owl looked down on him with an unblinking, all-knowing stare.

The simple farmhouse was enclosed by a white picket fence and appeared so conventional, Noah's spirits rose. Beyond the fence, fields stretched. Part of the land was in pasture, the rest was being farmed. From his position he could see two fields where stubble left from the harvest waited to be plowed under.

"My grandfather farmed this land for years," Rhiannon said as they stood just outside the front gate, "but grandmother leases it now to other farmers."

He could see a wood, a distant ridge, and the reflective glimmer of the sun off a pond. Nothing remarkable. This land was being used for exactly what it should be. Unless someone wanted it for some sort of development, although he couldn't imagine what kind. Or unless . . .

"Has there ever been a mineral survey done?" he asked.

"I'm not sure. Coal is Virginia's main mineral resource, but there are no mines in this area."

"Still, it's something to look into," he said. "There must be records."

"There probably are, but most businesses and

all of the city government offices are closed and won't open up until next Tuesday."

"Why are things closed today? It's Friday."

"Hilary celebrates Halloween from five o'clock Thursday afternoon until midnight Monday night."

"That's the craziest thing I've ever heard."

"Really?" Her brow rose with incredulity. "I'm amazed, since you live in New York City."

"The craziness in New York makes sense."

Her lips quirked. "Making sense of things is important to you," she said gently. "I understand."

She took his hand, and they began to walk across a meadow still thick with grass. She touched him a lot, he thought, warily taking note of the warmth rippling through his bloodstream. He wasn't sure how to deal with his reaction to her. Over the years his relationships with women had been satisfying, and normal, he thought. But what he was feeling with Rhiannon exceeded the bounds of normalcy and shot straight into the extraordinary category.

Around them the air was crisp and clear. The trees had lost most of their leaves, but those remaining were gold and red. A rabbit hopped across their path, stopped, looked at Rhiannon, and smiled, then bounded off.

The rabbit hadn't smiled, Noah told himself firmly.

"It means a lot to Esme and Lavinia that you're here," she said. "Why haven't you ever come before?"

"I haven't stayed away deliberately. When I was younger, Esme and Lavinia visited us every year. Occasionally my mother made a trip here, but I was usually in school or at summer camp."

"Hilary was better than any camp for a child. It gave me a sense of place I very badly needed, and the same people were here year in and year out when I came."

Sunshine wove through her hair, layering gilt on gilt, and tinting her ivory skin a pale warm gold. "I'm sorry now I didn't come," he said thickly. "We might have met sooner if I had."

"We definitely would have," she said, her words sure and filled with meaning, her expression solemn.

He missed a step. Her hand tightened around his, steadying him. With effort he recalled what he had been talking about, and continued. "Once I entered into law school, there never seemed to be time."

"Now that you've been here, you won't want to leave," she said. "No other place will seem as wonderful."

He imagined a spell being cast would sound something like what he'd just heard. He stopped and turned to her. "You're definitely a witch."

"If I were a witch," she said softly, "I'd find a way to make you kiss me right this minute. For instance, I'd put my arms around you . . . like this."

His heart rate picked up as she stepped in close to him and slid her arms around his neck.

"And I'd press myself against you like this. . . ."

Heat wound in his stomach and into his loins, making him hurt with wanting her.

"Then I'd thread my fingers through your hair so that I could pull your head down like this. . . . And I'd raise my mouth until I could feel your breath on my lips and you could feel my breath on yours like this. . . ."

Each word she whispered created a loud explosion in his head.

"And then I'd wait . . . and hope . . ."

He crushed his mouth down on hers and felt himself begin to fall apart. This was witchery, there was no doubt about it. He didn't like the sensation of things being out of his control. But her lips were soft and yielding and seemed made for his. And just for a moment he allowed his need for her to outstrip his need to understand her power over him. He closed his hand around a fistful of golden hair and tilted her head to deepen the kiss. He rasped his tongue against hers, almost rocking back on his heels at the electric charge of hunger he received.

And then he took her with him down to the grass and the leaves.

The weight of his body on top of hers was exquisite, and without conscious thought she spread her legs apart so that his thighs rested inside hers. She'd been kissed by many men, but the intense heat of Noah's kiss had caught her off guard. In her entire life she'd never felt such an instant attraction for a man, so she understood that he was bound to affect her differently. And his kisses and caresses were exactly what she wanted. It was just that she hadn't bargained on the inability to catch her breath, or the flames that licked through her veins at the feel of the hard ridge of his desire pressed so intimately against her.

He slid his hand beneath her sweater and cupped his long fingers around her bare breast. When his thumb flicked across the nipple, she gasped and arched up to him.

"It's nice to know witches can get excited too," he murmured, showering kisses over her face.

"I'm only a woman."

He raised his head and looked down at her. "You're not *only* anything. You're *more* than anyone I've ever known. And I desire you more than I've ever desired anyone else."

"Good," she whispered, moving her hips restlessly as the ache low in her stomach grew. "That's what I wanted to happen."

He stiffened. Her words were a reminder and came just in time. For a while he'd been pulled into a whirling vortex where something or someone other than himself had charge over his life. The feeling, he realized, had been with him since yesterday. He hated the very idea of it, but he couldn't prevent himself from taking her nipple between his thumb and finger and rolling it until she cried out. "You bewitched me from the first, didn't you? And I'm sure you never had a doubt that you'd have your way."

Fiery sensations were making it difficult for her to think. "Not really," she said, barely hearing her own words.

"No one manipulates me, Rhiannon. Not even a witch."

His hand was still on her breast, caressing, molding, driving her wild. But through the haze of the heat and the fire of the flames, she somehow sensed that emotionally he was withdrawing from her. She reached up and took his face between her hands, trying to bring him back to her. "I'm not manipulating you, Noah. There's been something between us from the start. Didn't you feel it yesterday when we met? Can't you feel it now?"

He ground his hips into her. "Lord, yes."

His priorities were beginning to shift. Reason was dimming. Then something off to his left caught his eye. He looked and saw Graymalkin. He was on a lower branch of an oak tree, not a muscle twitching anywhere in his body. It was as if he had grown out of the wood.

A chill cooled Noah's ardor, and an eerie, unsettling feeling took over.

"What's wrong?" she asked breathlessly.

"Your cat's here."

She turned her head and whispered, "Graymalkin."

As if he'd heard, he jumped down from the tree and trotted toward them.

Noah sat up and wearily rubbed his face. "Does he need a ride home or will he just turn into a bat and fly back to town?"

Sitting up, she straightened her sweater. Graymalkin came to her and rubbed himself against her, purring softly. Stroking him absently, she gazed at Noah from beneath her lashes. At the moment he was angry and confused because he was a man used to dominating, a man used to being master of his own fate.

The two of them had reacted differently to their intense attraction. He comprehended with his mind, not his emotions. She was just the opposite. She had accepted their fantastic chemistry without worry or second thought, but he'd been dazed and was trying to come to terms with it.

She sympathized with him, and she wished she could help him, but she was very much afraid he was going to have to work it through alone.

"Graymalkin can ride home with us," she said.

Three

Early Saturday afternoon Noah surveyed the colorful scene in the town square with a jaded eye. He hadn't wanted to come to the carnival. However, after a futile attempt the afternoon before to contact the mayor or any other public official by phone from the farm, he had concluded reluctantly that the best place to find what passed for an official was at the carnival.

A headless horseman rode slowly by. Just before he drew even with Esme and Lavinia, he bent the top part of his body in a bow to them, sending them into peels of girlish giggles. Noah grinned indulgently. He'd never known his aunts to be anything but happy, and he wanted to keep it that way. Their delight in having their nephew with them today was apparent. For them, he concluded, he could put up with the insanity for a few hours.

He could even put up with their costumes as long as he refrained from delving too deeply for a hidden meaning. Esme and Lavinia, both wearing long Victorian dresses, were Lizzie Borden and her sister, Emma. Esme, as Lizzie, accessorized her outfit with a hatchet. Lavinia, as Emma, wore a halo.

As they made their way through the carnival, he saw kids bobbing for apples, a usual event at Halloween. But there was also the not so usual event of a unicorn ride, where children rode small horses that had horns strapped to the middle of their head. And, he noticed with disquiet, the high school science department had an astonishingly large display of shrunken heads. When he remembered to check on his aunts, he found Lavinia had drifted off and only Esme with her hatchet remained beside him.

A witch walked by dressed all in black with a tall, pointed hat and a large hairy mole by the side of her beaked nose. Noah couldn't help but silently applaud her. At least she was a *conventional* witch. A man would be able to tell instantly by her appearance what she was and would know to be wary. Not like a certain sexy, blue-eyed, blond-haired witch who blindsided him every time he saw her.

He glanced toward Rhiannon's house. There was no sign of anyone, not even a black cat. She and her familiars were probably out collecting bats' wings and eye of newt for potions, he thought grimly.

Noah brought his gaze back across the square, and when he got to the big granite horse statue, his eyes narrowed. Children were stuffing roses into the military-type boots that nestled in the stirrups. Something about the statue bothered him, but then, so did everything else in this town.

Where was she?

"Does Rhiannon usually come to the carnival?" he asked Esme.

"Of course, dear. Everyone does." She beamed at an Igor lumbering by.

"Nice to have you with us, Noah," Igor said, and passed on.

Noah started. The way complete strangers called out to him by name truly unnerved him. "Aunt Esme, have you ever noticed that all Rhiannon's clothes are black?"

"You know, I never realized that before, but I do believe you're right. It's most becoming, don't you think? Not everyone can wear black. I certainly never could, and as for Lavinia, black makes her look like she's passed on to her reward. Oh, dear, there she is now."

His heart skipped a beat. "Rhiannon?"

"No, dear. Lavinia. She's with Delores Whitfield. I better go over and see if she's heard who's won first place in the pumpkin pie contest."

"Wait. Do you know where I could find the mayor?"

Esme scanned the crowd. "I don't see him, but he rode by a few minutes ago. He was the headless horseman. You can't miss him. He's the one without a—"

"Head. Right."

What else had he expected? The townspeople were loose from their moorings, caught up in a maelstrom of lunacy. And at the center of all the extravagant foolishness was an uncannily serene, excessively witchy woman named Rhiannon. He was *glad* she wasn't around. It was best that he avoid her.

He turned, an unconscious frown on his face, and found himself staring into a pair of endlessly deep blue eyes that reflected a knowing kind of amusement.

"Hello, Noah. You don't look as if you're having a very good time."

Like a thirsty man, he drank in the sight of her. Her blond hair waved in perfect disorder around her beautiful face. The overlarge cowl collar of her black sweater made the neckline fall off one satiny shoulder. A gored suede skirt and high-heeled boots completed the outfit. The all-black outfit.

He took hold of his turbulent emotions and mentally worked with them until they were all in proper order and under control. "I came to talk to some people, not have a good time."

"Why should one activity preclude the other?" she asked with real interest. "Or are you able to do only one thing at a time?"

His frown deepened. "Are your familiars lurking nearby?"

"I beg your pardon?"

"Never mind. Aunt Esme and Aunt Lavinia showed me the letter they'd received from Clifford Montgomery, the lawyer. I tried to reach him at his office, but no one answered. Have you seen him? Is he here?"

"I doubt it. I haven't seen him for several days. He's visiting his mother in Raleigh."

"And missing the big Halloween weekend?"

She raised her brows at his sarcasm. "His mother's ill."

He was determined she wouldn't get the best of him. "How convenient."

"I imagine his mother doesn't think so. And I can guarantee that if Clifford knew you were here waiting to tangle with him, he'd prolong his visit. He's very much a small-town lawyer, not up to your weight at all."

He looked around, frustrated. "Makes sense, since this is very much a small town."

"*What* are you so angry about?"

Damn good question, he thought. Aloud, he said, "I just have a hard time understanding how everyone in a town can suspend reality for four days."

"What's so wrong with it? Most people would love the opportunity to forget the realities of their lives for even a few hours. In Hilary, we're lucky enough to be able to do it for four days."

"Okay, okay," he said. "I give up. It's no use arguing with you about this town. You live here. You're a part of the madness." Hell, he thought, for all he knew she could be the *cause* of it. "How many real estate agents sell land in Hilary?"

She accepted his change of subject without so much as a blink of an eye. "Not many. Two that I can think of. There's one over there." She nodded toward a Dracula, who was cheerfully selling cups of bloodred punch.

"Shall we go over?" he said.

She nodded. He'd said "we." He could have walked away and left her, Rhiannon thought, but he had included her. For now she was satisfied.

The Dracula gave them a toothy grin as they approached. "Hi, Rhiannon. Where's your costume?"

"She doesn't need one," Noah said. "She wears hers all the time."

Dracula cast Noah a puzzled look.

"Martin Richardson, meet Noah Braxton," Rhiannon said. "Martin, maybe a cup of your punch will improve his mood. I'll pay. I'm willing to try anything."

"Coming right up."

A pair of dominoes walked by. "Hi, Rhiannon. Hi, Noah."

"Hi, guys," Rhiannon called after them.

Martin handed Noah the cup of punch. "You're Esme and Lavinia's nephew, aren't you?"

"That's right. And you're a real estate agent, I understand."

"One of the top two in town," he said, then laughed heartily at his own joke.

Noah waited until the man's laughter had subsided. "I'd like to ask you a couple of questions about your business."

Martin looked surprised. "You want to talk about business? Now?" He glanced at Rhiannon.

She shrugged. "What can I tell you? He's from out of town."

Martin nodded. "New York. I heard." He looked back at Noah. "Are you thinking of settling here? I can show you some real choice property if you are."

"We're too strange for him," Rhiannon said.

"Strange?" He rolled his eyes. "Heaven help us, and you living in New York City too, Noah."

Noah decided to ignore Rhiannon's giggle. "Actually, Martin, I *am* interested in the land around here." He felt Rhiannon's startled gaze on him, and went on smoothly. "If not to live on, then for investment purposes. So, about those questions . . ."

"Shoot," Martin said good-naturedly, ladling out punch for a small elf and a large Friar Tuck. "I'd be glad to answer any questions I can."

"I've heard that certain pieces of land have suddenly increased in value. Can you think of any reason why this has happened?"

Martin clicked his fang mouthpiece, then brought his fangs down over his bottom lip in a gesture of thoughtfulness. Finally he said, "I couldn't really say. Maybe people have found out what we've known all along: Hilary is heaven on earth."

"Heaven." He nearly made a sarcastic comment, but a glance at Rhiannon forced him to change his mind. He refused to be predictable. "Has anyone expressed undue interest in the land east of here?"

"No. Actually, business is never brisk at the best of times. Why don't you talk to Louella Gibson? She's the other real estate person in town. How's the punch?"

"What?"

"The punch. Make it myself every year."

"And every year he adds another ingredient," Rhiannon said.

Noah took a tentative sip and said the expected. "It's very good."

Martin Richardson smiled so widely, the white Dracula makeup on his face cracked. "How about another cup?"

"No, thank you. I think I'll go find Louella Gibson." He eyed the assortment of weird and colorful people around him. "If by some chance I miss her and you see her, would you tell her to call me out at my aunts' place tonight or early tomorrow. I'll be leaving sometime in the morning."

"In the morning? Are you kidding?"

"Uh, no."

"Listen, if I were you, I'd think seriously about waiting to leave until Tuesday morning. We're expecting our legend to happen Monday night, and you wouldn't want to miss that."

"What legend?"

"*Ours*. The town's. At any rate, you'll know Louella as soon as you see her. She's Frankenstein's bride this year. Her hair looks like she stuck her finger in a light socket. As a matter of fact, now that I think about it, she probably did." The thought sent him off into another gale of laughter.

A slimy-looking Creature from the Black Lagoon came flip-flopping up. "A large punch, please."

Rhiannon took Noah's hand in hers and drew him away from the booth.

She was definitely a person who loved to touch, he thought, and he was very much afraid her touch was reaching deeper than skin level. He'd intended to maintain his distance from her, but she was so fascinating, and their surroundings were so absurd, he found all his hard edges melting away.

A magic show was in progress on one stage they passed. A short distance away, another stage held the hardware store owner, juggling ketchup-covered chain saws. The sign behind him read VIRGINIA CHAIN SAW MASSACRE.

In the next area the good citizens of Hilary were being offered the opportunity to throw a brick and knock the chief of police into a bubbling vat of oil. Another game featured "guillotining" the high school principal.

"The level of normalcy in this town is frightening," he murmured.

"You're looking at it from an outsider's point of view. It's really a very nice town. You should stay and get to know us. Oh, look, they're selling invisible creatures in that booth over there." She tugged at his hand, pulling him over to the booth where a hairy wolf man presided gaily over stacks of crayoned boxes. "How much?" she asked.

Wolf Man opened his mouth, let out a long, loud roar, then said, "A dollar."

"I'll take one."

"Wait a minute," Noah said, picking up one of the little boxes and opening it. "There's nothing in here."

"Of course not," Wolf Man said. "It's invisible. And it makes very little noise."

"It'll make a perfect companion for Graymalkin and Merlin," Rhiannon said. "I'll take it."

"You made the right choice," Wolf Man said. "It barely eats anything at all."

She opened her purse, but Noah stopped her. "I'll pay."

"Oh, but—"

"Please. It will make me very happy for you to have at least one pet that doesn't give me the creeps."

She leaned close to him and kissed his cheek. "Thank you. And it is for a good cause, you know. All the money raised at this carnival goes toward new uniforms for the high school band."

Wolf Man let out an enormous roar. "Next?"

They strolled along, hand in hand. They passed a finger-food booth where all the food resembled real fingers.

"I may never eat again," he said.

She laughed. "It's just spaghetti."

"Yes, but it *looks* like . . ."

"*Now* it does. It's the power of suggestion."

"Does that explain this town too?"

She jerked on his arm, catching him off balance so that he fell against her. "Loosen *up*, Noah. You're acting like a stuffy New York lawyer."

Her magical floral scent wrapped around him as if to bind him to her. It took a real effort to straighten away from her. "No one's ever called me stuffy before."

Her exotic eyes held glints of laughter. "I can't imagine why not."

Reluctantly he smiled. "Lord, you are a witch, aren't you?"

"You do have the strangest ideas. When are you going to kiss me again?"

Heat flared. "And you wonder why I think you're a witch. You don't ask are you going to kiss me, but when are you going to kiss me. You're giving yourself away, Rhiannon."

She laughed. "I guess I am being obvious, but I don't have a lot of time to talk you into staying."

"I wouldn't even try if I were you."

She smiled with a serenity that threatened his sanity. "But then, you're not me. Let's go through the House of Horrors."

"I thought I was in it."

• • •

"We want you to stay here at the carnival as long as you like tonight," Esme said, punctuating the air with her hatchet. "But we're rather tired, and Norman and Amy Little have said they'll drop us off on their way to their place."

"There's no need for that," Noah said. "I'm ready to go back with you now."

He felt Rhiannon move close to him and smooth her hand down the lapel of his cream-and-brown-tweed sports jacket. Touching him again.

"Stay a little while longer. We could walk over to my house, and I could make some coffee for us."

"Oh, yes, dear, do go," Lavinia said encouragingly, her halo bobbing.

"It will give us a chance to say good-bye," Rhiannon said softly.

Her words shocked him. These past few hours he'd allowed himself to be caught up in the pleasure of the surrounding absurdity. And in the pleasure of being with Rhiannon. And he'd forgotten that he would be driving home tomorrow.

He couldn't decide whether leaving Rhiannon was an act of bravery or of foolishness. But in either case, he knew he wouldn't forget her. She was seared into his memory, a woman of grace, mystery, and incredible sensuality. A little more time with her surely wouldn't hurt.

He looked at his two aunts. "If you're certain you don't mind."

"It's settled," Lavinia said. "You two go on, and we'll see you when you get home, Noah."

With a wave of good-bye and smiles that bestowed their blessings, the two sisters strolled off.

"I won't be long," Noah called after them, more as an assurance to himself than to them.

"They're lovely people," Rhiannon said. "It's a shame you can't extend your stay."

The air was cooler now, and he shrugged out of his sports jacket and placed it around her shoulders. It was the first time he'd seen her wearing a color other than black, and the lighter shade against her skin and hair seemed odd. They started off across the park, heading for her shop. "There's no chance I can stay longer." He smiled dryly. "New York doesn't recognize Halloween as a legal holiday."

"Really?"

The surprise in her voice made him grin. "I have a whole desk of work waiting for me when I get back. Besides, I've come to the conclusion I'll have more luck in New York finding out what's going on than I will here."

She slipped her arm in his. "How are you going to do that?"

There was something very right about having her hold his arm and walk close beside him. The thought gave him pause before he deliberately shook away the feeling of softening. "As soon as I get back, I'm going to put one of my people on the problem, using the computer. I want him to see if he can find out if any company or business is showing interest in this area. There could even be a highway in the proposal stage."

She nodded thoughtfully. "If that were true, and someone had advance information, they could stand to make a great deal of money."

"You know, I haven't been in Hilary long enough to get an accurate pulse of the town, but it seems to me that there are a lot of genuinely nice people living here."

"There are. They're also happy and content. That's why I can't imagine who could be behind this strange buying spree."

"You probably know the person."

She shook her head. "No one I know would hurt someone just to get his land."

"No one's been hurt," he reminded her, "and one man was scared straight out of alcoholism." He grinned. "I'm sure that in the long run, years were added to his life."

She gazed up at him. "Are you aware that you've begun to unbend in the short time you've been here?"

"I'm a skeptic by nature and a cynic by occupation and two days *anywhere* isn't going to change that."

"Come on. Admit it. I think you even had fun today."

"I suppose I did, in a bizarre sort of way."

She tilted her head in the way she had when she was considering something. "Bizarre is not necessarily bad."

"Obviously not. This town thrives on it."

"You could make a phone call to your office."

Her change of subject threw him. He stopped. "What?"

"You wouldn't have to drive all the way to New York to relay what you want done. You could stay here and call in your instructions."

For a moment he simply stared at her. The expression in her eyes was weaving magic and heat around him so that he wanted to do as she asked. How could she cast these spells on him, here, out in the open, with people all around them? And why in the hell did he let her?

Tearing his gaze away from hers, he drew a deep breath, attempting to cleanse the need of her from his body. As it happened, the first thing he saw was the statue, and it suddenly dawned on him why the damned thing had been bothering him. "That horse doesn't have a rider."

She followed his gaze. "No, he doesn't."

"The statue has boots in the stirrups, but it has no rider."

"The children hide Easter eggs in the boots."

"I've never seen a statue of *just* a horse."

"Well, as you've said, Hilary is unique."

"I didn't say unique."

"I think unique is a nice word."

"If there's a horse, there's always a rider."

"That's the usual way," she agreed.

"Why would any town erect a statue to commemorate a horse?"

"Actually, the people didn't. The statue is in honor of the Yankee soldier, John Miller, who saved our town during the Civil War. He rode through here ahead of his troops to warn the town that the general planned to take no prisoners."

Her calm, reasonable tone had begun to grate on his nerves. "Why did he do that?"

"John and his family lived in Baltimore, but before the war he'd visited some friends here and fallen in love with one of our young women, Priscilla Davenport. He couldn't stand the thought of her or the town being in danger."

"That's a charming story, and I can see why the town would want to remember him, but why just his horse? Why not him on his horse?"

"As grateful as the town was to John Miller, they were still Confederate, and the people here felt very strongly that they couldn't have a statue of a Yankee soldier sitting in the middle of their town."

He should have known. She took his hand and began walking. He was getting used to her taking his hand, he thought. It hardly affected him at all anymore.

She cast him a glance out of the corner of her eye. "Your aunts have told me that you get involved only with career-oriented, unsentimental, very realistic women and that they always have goals along with solid reasons for doing things."

He stumbled. As once before, she steadied him. "How in the hell do they know that?"

"Your mother discussed the matter with your aunts quite often."

That was a revelation to him. Although he'd introduced his mother to several of his women friends, she'd never betrayed her opinion of them.

"They sound perfect for you."

"You're not real," he muttered, shaking his head.

They were at her shop now, and she opened the front door. "I'm real," she said, turning her head and looking at him over her shoulder. "Stick around and I'll make you believe it."

They stepped into the shop, and he heard the click of the door being shut behind him. He immediately felt uneasy. And excited beyond belief.

A faint light streamed through the pale, shimmery material that curtained the back room. In the dimness the masks and the costumes took on a spectral appearance. He'd willingly walked in here with a witch, he thought. He had to be out of his mind.

Upstairs, Rhiannon found it hard to concentrate. With Merlin perched on her shoulder, she measured out the coffee and water into the coffeepot, picked up the cord, looked at the electrical outlet, dropped the cord. She didn't want to make coffee. She wanted to be near Noah. She wanted desperately to convince him to stay.

"I don't have much time left," she whispered. "Not much time at all. Fly away, Merlin." The owl flew to the top of the armoire.

From the sofa Noah watched the owl's flight. "He's very attached to you, isn't he?"

"To him, I'm family," she said, returning to his

side. "That first week when I didn't know whether or not he'd live, I force-fed him strained beef baby food every thirty minutes or so around the clock. I was very grateful that I was able to save him, but my motive wasn't to make him a pet. I thought that once he was older and could fly, he would want to leave. When the time came, though, he chose to stay with me. On occasion, he'll fly off, but he always comes back."

He understood. She had a magnetism that pulled at living things, making them want to be near her.

"We really haven't had a chance to get to know each other," she said softly, choosing to sit on top of the trunk and face him.

"No, I don't suppose we have." The idea that a man could know Rhiannon at all was a tantalizing, boggling thought. The possibility that he might be able to peel away the mystical, complicated layers of her to see what lay beneath was almost too powerful a temptation to resist. But it was also totally unrealistic, and as long as he remembered that, he'd be safe.

Graymalkin jumped into her lap. She stroked him for a moment, then gently dumped him on the floor. Without protest he bounded over to the front window, climbed out, and settled among the flowers in the window box.

"Will you let me know if you're able to find out what's behind the offers?" she asked.

He nodded.

"You don't need my address. Just send any information to Rhiannon, Hilary, Virginia. Edwina will make sure I get it."

The impersonality of corresponding with her through a letter seemed wrong. In fact, the finality of their conversation seemed all wrong. But she wasn't real, and he had to return to reality or lose his sanity.

"I'd appreciate it if you would keep an eye on Esme and Lavinia."

"I'd do that anyway."

"Nevertheless, I'll give you my number in New York in case something happens and you need to get in touch with me."

"That's very nice of you, but I'm sure I won't need to use it."

Dammit, he didn't want to leave. What was wrong with him? Merlin stared unblinkingly at him from atop the armoire. It was said that owls were harbingers of magic. Magic surrounded Rhiannon, but nothing had ever prepared him to deal with sleight-of-hand witchery or supernatural enchantment.

His life, both personal and professional, was a known quantity and imbued with the comfort of predictability. He enjoyed the long, hard hours he put in with his work, and there were never any curves, turns, or detours that unsettled. Or cat-like blue eyes that made him feel as if they could see inside him.

"I'd better go," he said, and rose to his feet.

She nodded understandingly, stood, and took his hand.

One more time, he thought, she was going to lead him. One last time. And he was relieved. In another minute he would be free of her.

In the center of the room he stopped and pulled her roughly into his arms. His mouth came down on hers, and great shudders of emotion ripped through him. Lord, how could he deprive himself of her? She was an enchantress who could set every cell in his body on fire.

"I'm leaving," he muttered harshly against her lips, savoring her taste.

Excitement drummed throughout her body. "I'm not stopping you." But she clung to him, as if by holding him tightly she could keep him with her.

"Aren't you?"

She fervently hoped she was, she thought. But she knew that if she admitted how much she wanted him to stay, she might frighten him away. He wanted an explanation, but for this she had no answers.

Noah had never run up against anything he couldn't manage, but the tight rein on his control was just a fragile thread away from completely disappearing. If he didn't break away now, he wouldn't be able to.

Painfully pulling gulps of air into his lungs, he tore free and stared down at her. Her eyes were luminous with desire and entreaty—a mixture so potent it was guaranteed to make a strong man weak at the knees. Half mad, he hung on to the sane part of his brain with all his might. He'd always been one to plan ahead, to weigh the consequences and decide whether or not an action would be in his best interest. To some it might seem a calculated way to live one's life. But he considered it self-preservation. Especially in this case.

"Good-bye, Rhiannon."

Deep in the night Rhiannon sat on her window seat, stroking Graymalkin, who lay on her lap. "He can't leave," she murmured. "He can't."

A silvery tear spilled out of her eye, ran down her cheek, and dropped onto the cat's gleaming black fur.

Graymalkin blinked, then turned his head to stare toward the east.

Four

A clear crystal ringing sound was waking Noah. He'd heard that sound before, he thought groggily, but remembering how little sleep he had gotten, he decided to figure out where later. The tinkling came again, pure and clear, low and musical, almost like a woman's voice.

Noah's eyes flew open, and he was greeted by the sight of Graymalkin outside the window on the sill, his usual self-assurance and lordly bearing evident in every line of his black-furred body.

"Damn cat," he muttered. "Go back to your mistress and tell her it's not going to work this time."

The cat blinked but didn't move.

Determined to ignore the cat, Noah rolled off the bed and headed for the bathroom and a shower. When he returned to the room, he was pleased to see the cat no longer at the window. Mind over matter. It worked every time.

In quick and efficient order he dressed and packed, then went in search of Esme and Lavinia. Instead of his aunts, he found a note.

"Dear Noah. We've gone to church, but we'll be home soon. Please don't leave until we get back."

Great. Just great. So much for his early start. He pursed his lips and gave the matter some consideration. He hadn't planned on having breakfast until he'd driven about fifty or sixty miles, but while he was waiting for his aunts, he might as well have breakfast.

He turned toward the refrigerator and froze. Graymalkin was perched outside the kitchen window. Noah grabbed up a dishrag and flicked it at the screen. "Get out of here! Go home!"

The cat leapt to the ground and disappeared.

Noah rolled his shoulders in an effort to relax the muscles. "Damn but that cat's a nuisance."

He prepared and lingered over a large breakfast, but an hour passed, then another, and Esme and Lavinia still hadn't returned. Restless, he got up and went out on the front porch. There, his restlessness turned to cold anger.

On the hood of his car, Graymalkin sat sphinxlike with utter stillness and patience.

Noah slammed back into the house.

Graymalkin was a witch in a cat's body. There was no other explanation for it. The damned cat was haunting him, there every time he turned around, and he was sick and tired of it.

He made an instant decision. Less than a minute later he emerged from the house—on the inside, a pressure cooker ready to explode, on the outside, a picture of perfect composure.

Graymalkin watched Noah's approach, his pale blue eyes giving nothing away.

Noah walked to the side of the car and opened the door. "Okay, cat. Let's go."

Graymalkin jumped gracefully to the ground, trotted around to the open door, and leapt in. He settled himself in the exact center of the backseat, and Noah was left feeling like a chauffeur.

In town Noah brought his car to a screeching halt in front of Illusions, and reached in the back to scoop up the cat with one hand. Surprisingly Graymalkin gave no protest.

He found Rhiannon upstairs in her apartment, wearing her black silk kimono and sitting at the kitchen table.

She looked up, and a slow smile spread over her face. "Did Graymalkin pay you a visit again?"

Her obvious pleasure at seeing him did nothing to soothe his nerves. Without ceremony he plunked the cat down on the floor. Graymalkin ran across the room and leapt out an open back window.

Noah went pale. "Your cat just flew out a second-story window."

"There's a tree out there. He jumped to the tree. Are you all right?"

"You know very well I'm not," he said, inflecting each word with a biting emphasis. "You sent that animal to get me this morning."

"Noah, didn't you get any sleep last night?"

He ran his hand around the back of his neck. He supposed it had finally happened. He'd stayed too long, and now he was coming apart at the seams. "No, not much."

"Would you like a cup of coffee?"

"What I'd like is to be left alone. I'd like to be able to go to bed at night and wake up in the morning without seeing your damned familiar at the window."

She lifted her coffee cup to her lips and took a sip. "I don't see any problem with that since you're leaving today."

"That's right." He jabbed a finger at her. "And let me tell you something. If I see him *anywhere* in New York City, he's going to be one dead cat."

She crunched delicately on a piece of toast. "Be careful. You wouldn't want to harm an innocent cat. There are bound to be a lot of black cats in the city who look just like Graymalkin."

"I could spot that cat of yours in a dark alley. I could pick him out of a lineup of fifty black cats."

"A lineup, Noah?"

His teeth came together. "No other cat in the world has eyes like his."

"They are unusual, aren't they?"

"They're exactly like yours."

"Noah, are you sure you wouldn't like a cup of coffee?"

His gaze followed the wave of her hand over the kitchen table, and a chill slid through him. "Why is that table set for two?"

"I was hoping you'd come for breakfast this morning."

"There was no reason for you to think that. We said good-bye last night."

She shrugged, and the black silk shifted over her breasts. "I said I was *hoping*. Besides, a little positive thinking never hurt."

"So you set the table for two." He slowly shook his head. "You're not real. You and this bloody town simply aren't real."

Just for a moment he thought he saw hurt in her eyes. Then she stood and walked over to the stove, and he knew he'd been mistaken.

Rhiannon leaned against the stove, letting it support her weight. She'd experienced pain before, but never anything like this intense ache deep inside her that left her feeling weak and wounded. He didn't want to have anything to do with either her or the town she loved so much. He couldn't understand the peace and the charm she saw in Hilary, and the unique way it allowed its residents to be free. And he couldn't understand the rightness of the two of them being together.

"I've been doing things against my will ever since I've been here," he said, continuing.

She straightened and switched on the burner

beneath the coffee carafe. "It's got to have been awful for you," she said softly, her back still to him. "I'm sure it was very distressing for you, those times when you laughed out loud at the carnival. And it must have been terrible for you, having to hold me and kiss me—"

"Dammit, you know that's not true. It's just that . . ." He exhaled heavily. "Rhiannon, turn around and look at me. Please."

She switched off the burner, threw a glance at him over her shoulder, then crossed to the bedroom area and the armoire. "You sound like you're about to apologize, and I wish you wouldn't. There's really no need." She drew out a pair of black jeans and an oversize black turtleneck sweater and disappeared behind the screen.

Unwilling to raise his voice to ensure she heard him, Noah followed her into the bedroom area. From atop the armoire Merlin tracked his progress. When Noah stopped a few feet from the screen, Merlin's lids slowly dropped over his eyes.

Noah forced his gaze away from the owl. "Rhiannon, you took what I said wrong."

"You said everything you've done has been against your will. I don't know how I could have interpreted that any other way."

He groaned with the frustration of a man trying to capture a handful of stardust. To do so was impossible—just like this whole damned situation. "Try to understand. Two days ago I drove into a town that by anyone's standards has a serious mental health problem. Then I'm led by a cat to a shop, and find objects that turn into other objects and costumes that ambush people. The cat not only steals from me, but he won't leave me alone. And then there's you. I've never known anyone like you."

She emerged dressed from behind the screen and leveled a cool gaze on him. "Maybe you haven't. And maybe that's why you're so unnerved. On the other hand, you need to consider that maybe you're unnerved because of the way we affect each other. Either way, it's not my fault."

"Isn't it?"

Neither spoke, and the silence between them grew more and more solid, forming a wall of separation. Their division had almost solidified by the time she spoke.

"Have a good trip back, Noah."

She started past him, but he grabbed her arm. "Where are you going?"

Her hair swished across her shoulder as she looked up at him. "I have to go over to the school. There's a baseball game there this afternoon."

"What baseball game?" He didn't care about a damned baseball game. He just wanted to keep her beside him a little longer. Which was crazy.

"The afternoon after the carnival and before Halloween, we always have a baseball game between the 'good guys' and the 'bad guys.' The game starts at two. Everyone has a great time. But then, you won't be here, will you?"

He ignored her pointed remark and tried to think of another question. "Who makes up the teams?"

"Spider Man, the Incredible Hulk, Batman and Robin, Casper the Friendly Ghost, Godzilla, King Kong, and people like that play for the 'good guys.' The team of 'bad guys' is made up of Octopusman, the Skeleton, Rodan—"

"Rodan?"

"He's a very famous pterodactyl. Dracula, the Creature from the Black Lagoon, the Wolf Man, and several others will also be playing for the 'bad guys.' "

He realized he understood the concept behind the game, and felt as if he'd achieved a small personal victory. "Okay, so why do you have to go so early?"

"I'm the umpire, and I want to make sure everything's set up."

"Umpire?" He released her arm, the feeling of victory disappearing. Rhiannon as an umpire was a concept beyond his grasp. "May I use your phone?"

"Sure." She gestured toward the phone on the kitchen counter.

"Thank you. Esme and Lavinia went to church this morning and weren't back when I left. I don't want them to worry about me." He went to the phone and dialed his aunts. Esme answered and he told her where he was.

"That's fine, dear," she said. "We saw your bags and knew you hadn't gone far."

"I shouldn't be much longer."

"Why don't you stay in town, and we'll meet up with you there. We just have to change our clothes and then we're going to drive in for the baseball game."

He frowned. "You like baseball?"

"We never miss a game."

He glanced at Rhiannon. Merlin had perched on her shoulder, and she was gently stroking his feathers and speaking to him in a low murmur. *Co-conspirators.* He refused to accept the notion.

"Aunt Esme, do you know if the mayor will be at the game this afternoon?"

"Of course, dear, he plays for the 'bad guys.' "

"I see." The Headless Horseman was a bad guy. It made sense. "Well, do you know where he'd be right now?"

"Probably at Blue's Diner, dear, there on the square. He always eats lunch at Blue's."

"All right, I think I'll see if I can have a talk with him, then I'll meet you at the game."

"Does this mean you're not leaving today, dear?"

He hesitated as the revelation hit him that he really wasn't going to leave today. Amazingly, his mind had been working against him without his knowledge. He sighed and wondered what resources were left to a person once his mind had turned against him. "I guess that's what it means. I'll see you at the game."

He hung up the phone and glanced at Rhiannon. Both the owl and woman were staring at him. "I'm staying another day."

"I'm sure Esme and Lavinia will be pleased," she said cooly. "I'll walk you out."

This time she didn't take his hand, and he felt a disappointment he couldn't explain.

Blue's Diner turned out to be named after its proprietor, Jeremiah Blue, an extremely plump man who had costumed himself as Gainsborough's "Blue Boy." The masquerade was, in Noah's opinion, far from successful. For one thing, Jeremiah's costume was about two sizes too small. At the last booth in the back of the diner Noah found the mayor, attired in his Headless Horseman dress, with Martin Richardson, decked out in his Dracula garb.

Martin looked up at him and started with surprise. "I'd expected you to be long gone by now, Noah."

"Circumstances conspired against me," he said dryly. "I'll try again tomorrow."

The mayor's costume was built so that its shoulders rested over the mayor's head and he looked out between the lapels of the cloak. "We're mighty pleased to have you another day, Noah. You're not going to be sorry you stayed to see the game."

Noah looked down at his clothing. It had suddenly occurred to him that he was the only person roaming around town who wasn't wearing a costume—Rhiannon didn't count. When he'd first come to town, he'd viewed himself as the only normal person in the asylum. Now he was beginning to wonder if he could possibly be the only abnormal person.

"Actually," he said, "I was wondering if I might have a word with you, Mr. Mayor."

"Call me Jerry. And sure you can. Here, I'll just scoot over—"

Martin held up his hand. "I have to leave anyway. I need to go over and check to make sure we've got enough punch for this afternoon." He slid out of the booth, stood, and rearranged his long black cape around him. "See you at the game, Jerry. Noah, try to make it."

"I'll be there," he said, thinking Hilary had to hold the world's record for the largest concentration of cheerful people in one town. Or so it appeared. He still retained a large portion of his skepticism and would continue to do so until he found out if his aunts had reason to be uneasy. Until he did, it would pay to be cautious.

He took a seat across from the mayor and got right to the point. "I know that the courthouse is closed for the, uh, holiday, but I'm extremely interested in the land on the east side of town."

"Out by your aunts' place, huh?"

"That's right."

"Thinking of settling here?" the mayor asked, his voice bright with enthusiasm.

Noah found it hard to lie outright to a man who could maintain such a sunny disposition while clothed in such an uncomfortable-looking costume. He hedged. "Land is always a good investment."

"Well, you're sure right there, son."

"I'm interested in finding out if there have been any mineral surveys done on that land in, say, the last five years. Also, I'd like to have a look at the plat book of the area. I suppose all of those records are at the county seat, though?"

The mayor tried to nod, but his effort made it appear as if the upper part of the cloak had gone into a spasm. He finally settled for a simple "Yes."

It would pay him to take a few extra hours tomorrow and detour through the county seat, Noah reflected. Shouldn't be too much out of his way . . .

"Of course," the mayor said, continuing, "we keep a few records on hand, too, as a courtesy to our people. It's more convenient for them, and it helps me keep an eye on things around here."

Noah's gaze sharpened. "Would you have those particular records I mentioned?"

The cloak spasmed again.

For a moment the elation of having the information so close at hand made him forget what town he was in. Then he remembered. "But I'd have to wait until Tuesday morning, wouldn't I?"

"Well, now, I have a little time before I have to be over at the playing field. Why don't I just take you over there, show you where things are, and you can browse to your heart's content. You can lock up when you're through."

"What?" He wasn't sure he'd heard right.

The mayor let out a loud laugh at the stunned expression on Noah's face. "Well, why not? You're a lawyer, aren't you? A genuine, bonafide officer of the court. And, to top it off, you're Esme and Lavinia's nephew. I even had a crush on your mother when we were in the sixth grade. Cutest little thing you ever saw." He laughed again. "If I can't trust you, I'd like to know who I could trust."

Fifteen minutes later Noah was alone in the records department of the courthouse, the information he'd requested in front of him. If he stayed in this town until he was old and gray, he thought, he'd never get used to it.

With a grin he put his amazement aside and bent to study the plats. He knew that the sales hadn't closed on the properties of the three people who had agreed to sell, so there'd be no record yet of the new owners. But if anyone did have plans for some sort of development, he reasoned, they would set their sights first on the easiest parcels to buy—the undeveloped parcels. Unfortunately, he found the same names listed as owners now for the land in question as three years earlier and even twenty years earlier.

The mineral survey proved another dead end. The last one had been done over eighteen years before. Somewhat discouraged, he put everything away and locked up as the mayor had instructed.

Outside, on the courthouse steps, he paused. The square was practically deserted, and the few people remaining were all heading in the direction of the school.

Glancing down at the tips of his brown Italian loafers, he absently noted they needed a shine. A frown formed on his face as he studied his shoes. What was he doing? Killing time? Making a statement when there was no one to see him? *Stupid, Noah.* He'd told his aunts he'd meet them at the game, and he fully intended to do so. Besides, the last time he'd attended a ball game, he'd been in high school. One more afternoon away from the rat race wouldn't hurt anything, and, in fact, would probably do him good.

And Rhiannon would be there . . . umpiring.

A low, mournful sound came from across the street. Curious, he raised his head. Two pairs of eyes stared fixedly at him. Graymalkin and Merlin— side by side on a limb of a big elm tree.

Suddenly the absurdity of the situation hit Noah, and he burst out laughing. "Take the afternoon off fellows. I'm going." Still laughing, Noah headed for the school.

The bleachers were full by the time he arrived. A buxomy Elvira, along with Frankenstein's bride, was leading cheers. Dracula had a young lovely bent over his arm, his teeth at her neck. Godzilla and the Creature from the Black Lagoon, obviously the respective captains for the "good guys" and the "bad guys," were having a heated discussion out in center field. The bases, Noah noticed, were "dead bodies."

He spotted Esme and Lavinia in the stands and waved to them, but he was drawn toward Rhiannon. She was standing at the edge of the field, holding a golden-haired Princess Leia in her arms.

He didn't need her wary expression as she watched him approach to remind him of the tense way they had parted. But he was acting on a gnawing need to be close to her in some way, and since touching her physically was out of the question, he'd settle for speaking with her. But when he reached her, he couldn't believe what he said. "Why is Godzilla with the 'good guys?' Didn't he destroy Tokyo?"

When she didn't immediately answer, his heart sank. He wasn't sure what he wanted from her— maybe just a smile would do. She'd tied him in knots, but he couldn't leave town with things so stiff and awkward between them.

"Yes," she finally said, "but later he battled Rodan and that makes him good."

"Yeah, he fought Gamera and Mothra too," the little girl said.

For Princess Leia, Rhiannon had a smile. "Don't forget Monster Zero."

Princess Leia took pity on him and explained, "Monster Zero is a dragon with three heads."

"And that's good?" Noah asked.

Two blond heads nodded at him.

"And after Tokyo was rebuilt," Rhiannon said, "Godzilla went back and bought a whole chain of fast-food restaurants."

Princess Leia and Noah both regarded her with patent disbelief.

Rhiannon winked at the little girl in her arms. "Then again, maybe not. Oops, the game's about to start." She lowered Princess Leia to the ground, and as the child ran to the stands, she started walking toward home plate.

He grabbed her arm, but a cool look from her made him quickly release her. "Will I see you after the game?"

"I'm not the one who's leaving town, Noah." With that, Rhiannon, upset and hurting, went to take up her position.

And Noah, confused and aching, climbed the stadium steps to his aunts.

Bizarre didn't adequately describe the baseball game that followed, but Noah eventually found himself laughing, cheering, and in general having one of the best afternoons of his life.

Godzilla and the Creature from the Black Lagoon flipped to see who would be at bat first and the "bad guys" won. Batman was the pitcher for the "good guys," Robin, the Boy Wonder, the catcher. When the "bad guys" took the field, Octopusman, who played center field, turned out to be a secret weapon. He'd equipped two of his arms with extensions that reached eight feet and had large suction cups on the end. At one point Godzilla hit Rodan over the head with a baseball bat. Casper the Friendly Ghost, tripped on his sheet while running for a ball.

As the afternoon progressed, tension mounted until at the bottom of the ninth inning, with the score ten to nine, the "good guys," trailing by a point, came up to bat. The Wolf Man was on the mound, King Kong was at bat, and Frankenstein was behind home plate as catcher. The Wolf Man gave a roar and lobbed a pitch over the plate. King Kong swung and missed.

"Strike one," Rhiannon yelled out.

Beside Noah, Lavinia anxiously twisted a lace handkerchief. "King Kong's just got to come through."

"Knock it out of the park," Esme shouted encouragingly.

The Wolf Man wound up again and threw a slider that crossed the plate at King Kong's knees.

"Strike two," Rhiannon called.

Lavinia nudged Noah in the ribs. "Good call."

King Kong threw down his bat, planted his huge, hairy fists on his hips, and glowered at Wolf Man.

Rhiannon soothingly rubbed King Kong's woolly back and spoke a few private words to him. After a minute, the giant ape retrieved the bat and the game continued.

The Wolf Man let out a loud roar, wound up, and threw a knuckleball. The ball wobbled, wiggled, curled up and out, and did everything but travel a straight line, but by the time it got to the plate it was in the right place, and King Kong swung. With a resounding crack the ball arced toward center field.

Everyone in the stadium, including Noah, held his breath as he followed the ball's path. In the dugout, Godzilla anxiously chewed on his tail.

Octopusman kept his eyes on the flight pattern of the ball and backed until he could get one of his gloved hands beneath it. The ball came down right on course, but astonishingly it hit into Octopusman's glove, then bounced back out and started rolling. Octopusman tried to turn too fast and got tangled up in his arms.

In the meantime, King Kong had lumbered past first base.

Dracula started after the ball, his cape flying out behind him. The Creature from the Black Lagoon came flip-flopping in from the other direction. They collided in center field. The ball rolled between the Headless Horseman's legs, and Rodan scraped one of his wings on the ground trying to scoop up the ball as it went past him.

Everyone in the stands was on his feet by now, and King Kong had rounded third base. Finally the ball thudded to a stop against the fence, and the Skeleton scooped it up and threw it as hard as he could. Wolf Man made a daring leaping catch, then wheeled and hurled it to Frankenstein at home plate. The big monster caught it and reached out for a tag just as King Kong slid into the plate.

Rhiannon waited until the dust had cleared, then called, "*Safe.*"

Bedlam erupted. The "good guys" swarmed out of the dugout, and Batman and Godzilla lifted King Kong onto their shoulders. On the field, the "bad guys" crowded around Wolf Man to console him.

Tears streamed down Esme's cheeks. "That was the best game I ever saw."

"Me too," Lavinia muttered into her handkerchief, overcome by emotion.

"I agree," Noah said, putting his arms around his two aunts and giving each a hug.

Five

Noah waited until he saw Esme and Lavinia driving past him, then started up his car, backed out of his parking place, and followed them through the gathering dusk toward their farm. He could see them gesturing as they talked to each other, probably finishing the other's sentences as they usually did. It was an endearing habit his mother had once told him they'd had since they were girls.

He enjoyed being with them, he realized, and felt a little guilty that he hadn't spent much time with them since he'd been in town. He really should have arranged his schedule so he could have stayed longer. This one extra day wasn't enough.

A disquieting thought occurred to him. How much extra time would be enough for him? One week? Two? Three? How long would he have to stay here, he wondered, before he was ready to go back home and resume his sane, sensible life.

Sane and sensible, he repeated to himself. Funny how dull those two words sounded.

The red glow of the taillights in front of him blurred and faded as he remembered how well-wishers had crowded onto the baseball field, making it impossible for him to reach Rhiannon. He'd wanted to tell her how much he'd enjoyed the game and how wonderful she and everyone had been. He'd wanted to tell her he thought the lunacy had been inspired. He wanted to . . .

Hell. The game had nothing to do with why he wanted to see her. There was a hollow, dissatisfied feeling inside him, and he couldn't leave things the way they were between them.

He rubbed absently at his jaw. Maybe he'd stop by her house on the way out of town in the morning. Or perhaps he'd drive over tonight after dinner. A sudden unwelcome thought occurred. What if she wasn't home tonight? There might be some sort of post–ball game, pre-Halloween party he didn't know about. He'd ask Esme and Lavinia. They knew everything.

A black cat streaked across the road in front of his car. *Graymalkin.* He slammed on his brakes, and his car screeched to a halt.

A cold sweat broke out over his brow. Dear Lord, had he hit Graymalkin? He tried to organize his thoughts. Had he heard a cry of pain?

Had there really been a thud of a small body hitting the car, or had that been his imagination?

He thrust open the door and got out. His heart pumping with dread, he knelt and searched beneath the car, but to his surprise there was no sign of the cat. Puzzled and upset, he studied the surrounding area. He was at the edge of town, and luckily there wasn't too much traffic. Two cars had stopped behind him, and in the other direction he saw that Esme and Lavinia were turning around and coming back.

Frankenstein, the driver of one of the cars that had stopped, clomped up. "What's the matter, Noah?"

"I think I just hit Graymalkin."

"Rhiannon's cat?"

"Yes, but I can't find him."

"Is there any blood or fur on your car?"

"I didn't see any, but then, there's not much light."

Frankenstein rubbed at one of the bolts at his neck, giving the matter some thought. "I don't have a flashlight either, but listen, I wouldn't worry too much. You know what they say about cats—"

"What's that?" Spider Man asked, joining them, along with Elvira, Lavinia, and Esme.

"They have nine lives. I suspect Graymalkin has eighteen. He's special, that one."

"We're talking about Rhiannon's cat," Noah said to the newcomers by way of explanation. "I think it's possible that I hit him, but I can't find any sign of him."

Spider Man patted him on the back. "Don't worry. We'll all look up and down the road and see if we can spot anything."

With nods of agreement the little group spread out. Ten minutes later they were back together with nothing to report.

Noah thanked Frankenstein, Spider Man, and Elvira, then turned to his aunts. "I've got to go back into town and tell Rhiannon."

"Do what you think is best, dear," Esme said, "and don't worry about dinner."

"We were just going to heat up leftovers anyway," Lavinia said. "Stay with Rhiannon as long as you think it's necessary. If something has happened to Graymalkin, she's going to be heartbroken, but—"

"—I believe he's safe and sound. In fact, he's probably home."

Noah clung to his aunts' optimistic belief on the short trip back to Rhiannon's. His headlights caught her in their beam as he steered his car into a parking place in front of her shop.

Rhiannon heard the car pull up, and with her hand on the doorknob glanced over her shoulder. "Noah?" she whispered, afraid to believe he was really there.

She'd just been mentally berating herself for being so cool toward him at the game. Her only defense was that she hadn't known how to deal with the pain of his good-bye, and she'd let it overwhelm her.

She'd searched for him after the game, but there'd been so many people on the field, she hadn't even been able to catch sight of him. In the end she'd decided he had gone without caring that matters had been left unresolved between them. Now, though, excitement speeded her pulse.

He jumped out of the car and bounded up to her. "Have you seen Graymalkin?"

Her spirits plummeted. He hadn't come to see her after all. What had Graymalkin done now, she wondered wearily. "No. Why?"

"Just now, at the edge of town, he darted in front of my car. I may have hit him."

"Graymalkin?" Her eyes widened with dismay.

Confused, he touched his forehead. "I'm not sure what happened, but I think I heard him cry out. Or I heard a thump. I don't know. My mind was on something else." He reached out and gently took hold of her arms. "I'm sorry, Rhiannon."

"Where is he? Is he at the veterinarian's?"

"No. I don't know where he is."

"Wait a minute. You didn't find him?"

He shook his head. "There wasn't much light out there, but several people helped me search on either side of the road. Rhiannon, I keep picturing him out in a field somewhere, hurt. He didn't have to do it, you know. I was going to come back to see you."

As she listened to him, her mind slowly cleared,

and she realized he wasn't thinking straight. "Noah, you couldn't have hit him. If you had, you would have found him or some sign of him."

"But I *saw* him. He ran in front of my car."

"He may very well have. But he also probably kept right on running. Let's go upstairs and check for him. If he's not there, we'll get a couple of flashlights and go back out to the spot where you think you hit him. But I'm betting he's not anywhere near that area."

He drew his first deep breath since slamming on his brakes. Her calm and reason was making him feel better. "I hope to hell you're right. Graymalkin has haunted me ever since I've been in town, but if anything's happened to him, I'll never forgive myself."

Her face lightened. "You called him by his name. That's the first time."

An hour later, after a thorough but unsuccessful search for Graymalkin, Rhiannon emerged into the living area, damp and glowing from a bath, wrapped in her black silk kimono and that scent that never failed to excite Noah.

"Now I feel better," she murmured. "Umpiring can get pretty dirty. Ummm, you have a nice fire going."

He gave the log he'd just added a final jab and racked the fireplace poker. "Thanks. Witches aren't the only ones who can control the elements, I guess."

She grinned, glad to see he was no longer upset. "Apparently not. Can I get you something to drink? I'm going to have a brandy."

"That sounds good. I'll have the same." Deciding to leave the wing chair by the fireplace for her, he chose an easy chair that usually sat across the room and pushed it into position for himself. But when she returned, she handed him his drink and sank onto the floor, facing him, her back to the fire.

He took a healthy gulp of the brandy and immediately felt its strength and warmth. "I don't see Merlin. I suppose he's lurking somewhere nearby, ready to swoop the minute I let my guard down."

"He'd get really bored if he waited for that," she said dryly.

He stared at her over the crystal edge of the tumbler. "You've come closer to seeing me with my guard down than anyone."

She swallowed against the sudden dryness in her throat. "I'm sure Merlin's out with Graymalkin."

"I saw them together earlier today."

"See. They're together, trust me."

"I'd still like to stay here until he comes home, just to make sure he's all right. That is, if you wouldn't mind."

"You're welcome to stay as long as you like," she said softly.

The fire backlit her hair, diffusing its fiery glow through the beautifully disheveled blond strands. He used anger to counteract the effect the sight had on him. "When I see that damned cat of yours, I'm going to wring his neck."

Her lips quirked. "So we're back to 'that damned cat.' What happened to calling him Graymalkin?"

"We didn't find the slightest indication he'd even been in the area, and I'm now convinced I didn't hit him. That means he's alive, and that means he's 'that damned cat.' "

"Let me get this straight. You feel better because you didn't hit him. So you're going to kill him. And you want to stay here until he comes home just to make sure he's all right." She reached out and patted him on his knee, a gesture of support to a lunatic.

Her touch dissolved his anger and set his senses humming. He prescribed more of the brandy as a cure.

"I didn't see you after the game," she said, her tone deliberately casual. Nothing had really changed between them, and she had to remember that.

His cure hadn't worked. She was still the most bewitching woman he'd ever known. He wanted her almost beyond reason, and no amount of brandy was going to change that. He set the glass aside. Any minute now he would cease to fight against her. "I tried to reach you, but you were surrounded. It was a great game."

"I'm glad you got to see it."

"Is the game always so wild?"

"Always. It's hard to decide who has more fun, the players or the spectators. But in the end, everyone goes home in a wonderful mood."

"The losers probably don't."

"What losers? The ball game always ends in a tie, just like this year's."

"Every year?"

"Yes. No extra innings in the Halloween game."

He caught himself just as he was about to ask if she didn't think a record of all-tied games was a little strange. He was learning. Then again, maybe he wasn't, because he did have another question he knew he would regret asking. He did it anyway. "Did you make that ball jump out of Octopusman's glove?"

Her brows rose slightly. "*Noah*. You saw the same game as I did. You saw where everyone was positioned. I was behind home plate. Octopusman was in center field. Why would you think I had anything to do with it?"

He drew a hand across his forehead. "Oh, I don't know . . ."

"You were tired and overworked when you arrived here, and you haven't had much time to rest. You really should take better care of yourself."

Her sweet tone reached out and tied around him like a wide velvet ribbon. He gave up. "I never had any problems until I came to Hilary. But then, I've had a lot of new experiences since I've been here." He paused. "I've never met a witch before."

"I don't know where you got the idea I'm a witch," she said, feeling anything but all-powerful.

"So you say, but I don't know what else to call you. You have a way of being with me even when we're not together."

She tilted her head, sending her golden blond hair spilling over her shoulder. "What do you mean?"

"Remember I told you I was thinking of something else when Graymalkin darted in front of me?"

She nodded.

"I was thinking of you."

She felt her heart give a lurch, and she laughed nervously. "I'm not sure that's good. I've had the distinct impression that you have some pretty dark thoughts regarding me."

"Not dark. Just confused. I still am to a certain extent, but I've decided the only thing I can do is relax and enjoy the confusion, go with it, sort of like a leaf riding the current of a warm, sensual stream."

Her throat moved convulsively.

His gaze touched her throat, her lips, then her eyes. "I was planning on driving back in to see you tonight, but I was afraid you'd be out at a party."

"There are never any parties the night before Halloween."

"Resting up for the big day, right?"

She nodded.

"See there. I'm growing accustomed to the way people in this town think. But not you. I'm also beginning to understand that you were right when you said *bizarre* is not necessarily bad, and *unique* is a nice word."

She regarded him cautiously, unsure what he was telling her. "You say you're beginning to understand."

"Yes, although I admit I have a long way to go. My head is telling me to return to New York, my emotions are telling me to stay here and discover what new delights you have in store for me."

Her tongue darted out and moistened her bottom lip. "And what are you going to do?"

"For the first time in my life I'm going to go with my feelings." He reached down and pulled her to him so that she was kneeling in front of him.

She couldn't seem to find her breath. "Noah . . ."

He parted his knees and drew her closer to him. "I'm tired of fighting against the power you have over me. I'm surrendering. Totally and completely." He smiled, enjoying her astonishment. For once he was the one in control—no matter for how short a time. "So, Rhiannon, what do you have in store for me? What have you got planned? Whatever it is, I'll tell you right now I'm going to enjoy the hell out of it."

Heat spiraled through her, reaching to every part of her, melting away the stunned surprise that had been holding her immobile. She slid her

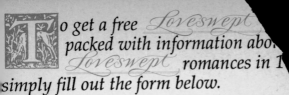

To get a free *Loveswept* packed with information abo *Loveswept* romances in 1 simply fill out the form below.

Calendar available early December, 1989. Offer g while supplies last.

Name _____

Address _____

City _____ State_____ Zip _____

Would you please give us the following information:

Did you buy Loveswept Golden Classics (on sale in June)?
____Yes ____No

If your answer is yes, did you buy __1 __2 __3 __4

Will you buy Golden Classics featuring Hometown Hunks on the covers?
I will buy 1-2____, 3-4 ____, All 6____ None____

How often would you like to have an opportunity to purchase Golden Classics?
Every month_____ If so, how many per month_____
Quarterly_____

* One calendar per household.

Be sure to get all the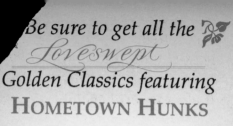

Loveswept

Golden Classics featuring

HOMETOWN HUNKS

On sale in October

---

arms around his neck. Like a circle of fire closing, at last their passion would know completion. "If I ever had any real plan—and I don't think I did—it just went right out the window."

He looked down at her. The black silk sash had come loose and her robe had parted, allowing him a view of her breasts and their rose-hued, stiffened tips. "Then let's improvise," he said gruffly, and ground his mouth down on hers.

A weakness flooded through her, and he took her weight against him. His tongue darted, plunged, then twined with hers, but he was the one seduced. She had a rare sensuality that provoked and inflamed. How could he go slowly with her? She was too sweet and soft, too yielding and ready. He knew with a sudden certainty that their joining would be like nothing he had ever known before. Impatience got the better of him, and he scooped her into his arms.

The bed gently rocked as he settled them onto it. "What's it like to make love on a bed that swings?" he asked, branding her skin with kisses.

"I don't know. I've never made love on this bed."

A question sprang into his mind, but she maneuvered out of her robe, and he forgot what he'd been going to ask.

She was an ivory goddess. The elegant, sensual lines of her body made his throat close with an aching need that shook him with its force. "You're the most glorious woman I've ever seen."

She drew his mouth down and kissed him. She'd

been right after all, she thought in a haze of happiness. Her instincts hadn't failed her. Soon she would know his lovemaking, know the feel of him, the strength of him. And she would have all that she desired.

He slid his hand from the flat of her stomach up to the roundness of one firm breast. "Silk," he murmured, and bent to capture a delectable peak between his lips. The urge to absorb her drove him to pull and tease at the sweetness of the nipple.

She moaned, and her hips lifted. "You know what?" she asked huskily. "I like improvising."

"Good, because I have a feeling we're going to be doing a lot of it." With his mouth still at her breast, he skimmed his hand to between her legs. "If you're silk on the outside, what are you like on the inside?" he muttered, letting his fingers explore. She cried out, and he put his mouth over hers, catching all sound, all breath, and replacing it with his own. "You're like dark velvet," he said, answering his question. "Moist, soft, infinitely desirable."

The intimacy of the act robbed her of coherent thought. He was caressing her as if he knew everything about her. A knot of tension formed low in her stomach, growing tighter and larger. "Noah . . ."

He rubbed his lips back and forth across hers, all the while probing and stroking with his hand. Then he raised his head, looked down at her, and was mesmerized by the wonder he saw in her eyes. "Lord, Rhiannon, I want you."

She felt as if she would burst with the feelings inside her. Surely the culmination would come soon.

He muttered an oath and left her. The bed swayed violently as he pushed off it and stripped out of his clothes.

Bereft and in an agony without him, she lifted her arms to him. "Come back."

It was an invitation, an order, a spell, and it had him trembling.

He came down on top of her and entered her, almost in the same motion. The resistance he met and its implication reached his brain after the fact. Shocked, he went still.

"You're a virgin?"

Not even a glimmer of concern or uncertainty showed in her eyes. "Of course," she said softly, "but don't worry. It's all right."

The bed moved back and forth, but he remained motionless inside her. Nerves clamored wildly for release, but he had to know. "Why me, Rhiannon?"

She wrapped her legs around his hips. Why was he wasting time talking? How could he even think? "Because I knew it was right."

Her muscles quivered and pulsed around him until he could stand it no longer. He thrust into her, at first slow and shallow, then, as her cries of ecstasy grew, deeper and harder.

The fever built; time and control ceased. They

moved together in wild abandon, fused by a rapturous passion that had no boundaries.

There was only urgency and feelings so intense they were unbearable. Together they escaped to a level of ecstasy neither had known existed, and their relief came, shatteringly powerful.

Clouds of sleep gently parted. Rhiannon stirred and encountered hard arms encircling her. Memories of the past hours she'd spent with Noah drifted slowly back to her, until she came awake and remembered everything.

A glowing satisfaction permeated her body; she felt soft and warm. But a small ripple of disquiet slipped into her consciousness, where it lingered, disturbing her tranquility. She searched her mind for what could be wrong, but found no answers.

Maybe if Noah weren't so close she could think better. His body was a continuous line of contact and heat against her back, and she discovered to her dismay that she still wanted him.

Behind her, Noah gave in to the temptation he'd been feeling for the last ten minutes and lightly stroked his fingers through the softness of her blond curls. The line of his lips took on a gentleness. At least this time he knew her hair had been disheveled by lovemaking and sleep and not wind. "Are you awake?" he whispered.

Her pulses jumped at the sound of his voice. Slowly she rolled onto her back and gazed up at him. The lines of his stern face had relaxed and made him appear even more handsome, she thought. Had making love to her done that to him? And if so, what changes had their lovemaking wrought in her?

"How do you feel?" he asked. "I tried not to hurt you, but by the time I realized, it was too late for me to pull back."

She didn't want him to feel guilty about something that was her fault, and she put a finger against his lips. "I feel wonderful. And you didn't hurt me."

He smiled tenderly. "I can't believe you waited for me. The fact that you did makes what we just shared all the more special. I feel like the luckiest man in the world."

"It was more than special," she said, wonder and confusion mixing in her voice. How could something so extraordinary make her feel so uneasy? "But—" Suddenly she went still.

"What is it?"

"Shhh. Listen."

Noah heard the clip-clop sound of a horse's hooves striking the brick street. "Who could be out riding at this time of night?"

The intrusion of the familiar into her sense of apprehension made her relax. "It's just one of Hilary's teenage citizens, pulling a little prank. Every year one or more of them decides to get a jump on John Miller and help our legend along. They have a great time trying to fool people, and they usually do it even during the years the roses don't bloom."

It was hard to concentrate on anything other than her warm, naked body against his, but there'd been too many mentions of the legend that he'd let pass. He rose and went to the window. Sure enough, a jeans-clad young man with a pumpkin under his arm and a big smile on his face was guiding his horse around the square. In the shadows of the buildings, Noah could make out several of the boy's friends, running to keep pace with him.

He turned back to her. "What is this damned legend everyone talks about?"

For a minute she couldn't speak. The moonlight washed his body in pale silver, highlighting sinews and muscles, dramatizing the power she'd experienced in such an intimate way. She felt herself turn warm at the memory.

"Come back to bed, and I'll tell you."

The desire he heard in her voice took him by surprise. He joined her, and after arranging the pillows beneath their heads, gathered her against him and kissed her long and deep. "I'm not sure I care about the legend anymore," he said.

She smiled, feeling the same way. But he was back in bed with her, holding her, and for the moment she was content. "You already know part of it anyway. I told you about John Miller and how he fell in love with Priscilla Davenport before the war."

He nodded and wound one of her silky blond curls around is finger.

"Well, the night he rode through here to warn the town, he took Priscilla into his arms and confessed his love for her."

"Is that according to actual eyewitness accounts?"

She giggled, and Noah felt a surge of pride that this extraordinary creature was his.

"That night he promised to come back for her as soon as the war was over. But the war stretched on, and Priscilla came down with a fever and died."

"Oh, no."

She grinned at his mock dismay. "That's what John Miller said when he was finally able to return. It was the night of October thirty-first, and he'd brought her a bouquet of roses. When he was told the news of her death, he wandered off, heartsick. He dropped the roses on the very spot where the roses grow wild today. A short time later, news was received that he had died."

"Let me guess. His horse threw him."

"No. He died of a broken heart."

"Darn. How could I have missed that one?"

"Then one October thirty-first, at around midnight, they heard him riding his horse down the street. Poor soul, he was looking for Priscilla."

"And I gather he's still looking for her?"

She nodded. "He doesn't come every year, and he doesn't always come exactly on the thirty-first.

Sometimes it's the night before, sometimes the night after."

"Where is he when he doesn't show up here?"

"No one knows, but when the roses bloom, as they are this year, he always comes to Hilary."

He was almost afraid to ask his next question. "Have you ever seen him?"

"No, but I've heard him."

"Other people have seen him?"

"Yes, off and on through the years. Or so they say. I've never known anyone who's actually claimed to see him."

"Rhiannon—"

"I know. You think it's crazy because it can't be explained rationally."

"If I'd been living in Hilary all these years, and I'd heard him, I would have gotten up and looked."

"Try to see it from our point of view. What would happen if I or someone else looked and didn't see him? The whole town would be devastated." He shook his head and she knew she wasn't getting through to him. "Do you remember how disappointed you were when you found out there was no Santa Claus?"

"I wasn't disappointed. I was relieved. Santa Claus never made sense to me."

She felt the pang of disquiet again and attempted to ignore it. "Then you're strange."

"Ah. And here I thought it was the town that was strange."

"I feel sorry for you."

His fingers stilled in her hair. "Me?"

"You've never known the joy of simply believing."

"There's always a logical explanation for everything, Rhiannon. Obviously there have been people through the years who have been more successful than that teenager down there at fooling the town."

The idea and the fact that he expressed it in such a serious tone struck her as funny. "Maybe the method is a secret that's been passed down from generation to generation through the same family," she said solemnly.

"Maybe—" He caught himself, realizing she was teasing him. He grinned. "Even in the moonlight I can see your eyes twinkle." He lay a caressing hand on her face. "I love you."

Her breath lodged in her throat, even as all the disturbing feelings came flooding back. But she had no time to examine the emotions because the next sensation she felt was heat as he took possession of her mouth and her body.

Six

Rhiannon closed her eyes against the morning light. There was something wrong. Sunlight had never bothered her before, but this morning it seemed too strong. Or maybe it was that she was too weak.

Noah's even breathing beside her was testament to the fact that he was still asleep. Why wasn't she? Their night had been exhausting. Wondrous.

Frightening.

She couldn't avoid it any longer. Slowly she opened her eyes, forcing herself to face both the light and the facts. Last night Noah had shown her a world where new types of hurts existed, where edges could be ragged, where sensations could be raw. She'd been stunned and unprepared for the violent emotions she'd felt during their lovemaking.

For years now she'd been cushioned from the heartache she'd known as a young girl by the security and love she'd received here in Hilary, and she'd forgotten there were other potential hurts and threats.

She'd singlemindedly focused on the moment when Noah would take her into his arms and make love to her. Because she'd never experienced real passion before, she'd thought their lovemaking would be a culmination of all the needs he had awakened in her. Instead, their lovemaking was an unknown beginning, and she was frightened. In her experience, changes meant hurt. The same instincts that had told her having Noah make love to her was right were now telling her to withdraw from him as fast as she could.

Carefully she rose so as not to disturb Noah, and went to take a bath.

When she returned, Noah was up and dressed. And Graymalkin was standing stone-still in the middle of the room, staring with wide eyes and puffed tail at the chair Noah had moved in front of the fireplace last night.

"He's back," Noah whispered, "but something's wrong with him."

"It's the chair. It's not in its usual position, so he's not sure what it is. Watch."

After a minute, Graymalkin cautiously approached the chair and circled it, examining it from all angles. Finally satisfied that the chair was one he knew, he relaxed and leapt out the front window to settle in the window box.

"Drawing back from the unknown is a feline trait," she explained. "Cats can take or leave people, but the things in their world have to be in order."

He went to her and wrapped his arms around her. "I'm going to have to learn about cats and owls, aren't I?"

He pressed a soft, gentle kiss to her mouth, and despite her fears and her questions, she could not remain unaffected by his lips on hers. Her body came to life with a heat and an aching need that intensified the turbulence inside her.

"Merlin is back too," he murmured, and gently drew away.

Rhiannon glanced over her shoulder to the armoire, where Merlin was perched, asleep. She hadn't noticed him. She really was slipping.

Noah smiled down at her. "Today's the big day, right?"

"Day?"

"*Halloween.* Did you forget?"

"No, of course not." But she had. Noah had obliterated everything but him from her mind. To her, it seemed a dangerous ability. "I'd better get dressed."

"So what happens today?"

She opened the armoire and chose a pair of black jeans and a black sweater. "Why? Don't tell me you're actually looking forward to it."

He shrugged. "I'm curious. I've never done Halloween in a big way before. What's the schedule?"

She retreated behind the screen and then had to question why. He'd spent hours last night learning her body. He'd covered every inch of her with kisses and caressed secret places to fiery life. Just exactly who was she trying to hide from? "Most people stay home this morning, preparing the treats they're going to give out this evening."

"Treats. That part sounds like fun. What are we going to make?"

We. Apparently he wasn't being beleaguered by doubts. "I've already made my treats. Cat-shaped cookies. The kids love them. They think the cookies look like Graymalkin."

"What does he think?"

"He thinks they're beneath his dignity. In fact, he ignores me during the time I'm giving them out." Dressed, she emerged from behind the screen.

Noah glanced at Graymalkin, who was curled contentedly among the flowers, enjoying the superior view the window box gave him of the square and his subjects. "Ummm. Have you explained to him the cookies are not a form of cannibalism?"

Yesterday she would have been delighted by his question. Today it only irritated. "You're speaking of him as if he's a person."

Her sharp tone caught his attention. "Is there something wrong?"

She folded her arms and hugged them tightly to her chest. There *was* something wrong, but it barely made sense to her. How could she explain it to him? "It's just that I'm not sure I understand what's happened here. Suddenly you're interested in Halloween, and you're speaking of Graymalkin as if you actually like him—"

"I wouldn't go as far as that," Noah muttered, casting another glance at the cat. This time the blue eyes were gazing back at him. Noah was the first to blink and look away.

"Why, Noah? Why are you suddenly a partici- pant instead of a critical observer?"

He reached for her and drew her back into his arms. "I told you last night. I've surrendered. I should have done it sooner, because I really never had a chance. How could I fight a spell cast by a beautiful, seductive witch?"

"A beautiful, seductive witch? You're being ri- diculous, Noah."

"I suppose being in love will make a man ridicu- lous," he said, and dropped a soft kiss onto her lips. "I don't know. I've never been in love before. So far, though, I'm having the time of my life." He broke away and started toward the phone. "I'd better call my aunts. I don't want them to worry. And then I'll call my office. You were right. I can give instructions from here."

She regarded him broodingly. "It sounds like you're planning on being here for a while."

He picked up the receiver and began dialing. "I can stay a few more days. After that, I'll have to get back. My law practice is there, and I can't just walk away from it, even if I want to. But when I leave, you're going with me."

His utter certainty made her want to gnash her teeth together. "Tell me, Noah, do I get a big red bow?"

"What?" He turned, startled. The phone was ringing in his ear, and he wasn't sure he'd heard right.

"It sounds as if you plan to wrap me up in a nice, neat package to take back to New York with you."

"Where did you get that idea?" The phone was picked up on the other end, diverting him. "Aunt Esme? Is that you?"

"Yes, dear," she said, hiccuping. "Did you dial the wrong number?"

"No. I meant to call you."

"Then it worked out well"—she hiccuped again— "didn't it?"

"Yes. Aunt Esme, are you all right? You sound . . . strange. What's that noise I hear?"

She hiccuped. "Noise?" She giggled. "Oh, we're just playing a little music, dear. The radio announcer said it was ZZTop. Nice beat. Good for dancing."

He frowned. "Maybe you'd better put Aunt Lavinia on the phone."

"No." She laughed, then hiccuped. "She's busy."

"Aunt Esme, have you been drinking?"

"Goodness no. Mind you, we're not teetotalers, not like your great-aunt Amanda, but after all"

—she hiccuped—"it's only ten o'clock in the morning." She giggled.

"Aunt Esme, what are you doing?"

"We're baking, dear. It was nice of you to call, but I've got to go now. Good-bye."

"No, wait—" He heard the click as the line was disconnected. "Dammit." He hung up the receiver and looked at Rhiannon, who'd come to stand beside him. "Something's wrong."

Her own worries were forgotten. "So I heard. What do you think it is?"

"I don't know, but we'd better go out and check. Too many unexplained things have been happening out that way lately."

"Let's go."

"Wait a minute. What were you saying about a nice neat package?"

Her hesitation was only for a moment. "Nothing that can't wait."

"I don't believe this," he muttered, gazing with amazement at the sight before him.

"Believe it," Rhiannon said beside him, a wide grin on her face. "Your aunts are high on sugar."

At the counter, Esme worked the electric mixer, gaily dumping powdered sugar into the mixing bowl. The sugar hit the beaters and blew back out, so that powdered sugar hung thick in the air and covered every surface. Lavinia, pastry tube in her hand, was slumped at the table, staring with fascination at the pulse in her wrist. The radio played rock music at full volume.

He walked over to the radio and switched it off.

Lavinia continued to study her pulse.

Esme glanced vaguely around. "Hel-looo there. I could have sworn we just talked on the phone. Rhiannon, don't you look pretty. I wish I could wear black as well as you do."

"Thank you, Esme," she said, walking to her side. "What are you making?"

"Pumpkins." She grinned, then hiccuped. "We made a whole passel of chocolate sponge sheet cakes and cut them into little circles. I'm in charge of putting on the orange fondant glaze, and Lavinia's in charge of the decorating. Lavinia?"

Lavinia spoke without looking away from her wrist. "You know, it's the strangest thing. I never knew you could actually *see* your pulse like this. Come look at my pulse, Esme. It's most amazing."

"I will later. Noah and Rhiannon are here." With that announcement, she began laughing.

Noah unplugged the mixer. "We need to get them out of here."

Lavinia roused herself. "I have too much work to do to go anywhere."

Rhiannon walked over to the table and bent to inspect the lopsided, drunken-looking pumpkin faces Lavinia had been decorating. Some had smiles on their faces, some frowns. One had three eyes. "You've done a wonderful job," she said enthusiastically. "The children will love them."

"Do you really think so?"

"Absolutely. And you've already done most of them. It's not going to hurt anything to take a little break." She put her hands beneath Lavinia's elbows and helped her up. "Why don't we all go out to the front porch and breathe in some fresh air."

Across the room Noah gently guided Esme toward the door. "Her skin is coated with sugar," he muttered.

"Powdered sugar is baker's cocaine," Lavinia chanted in a rap-song rhythm.

Out on the porch Noah and Rhiannon settled the two ladies into chairs and brushed them down as well as they could. Rhiannon returned to the kitchen and quickly prepared a plate of cheese and crackers. "Protein should help," she said, back outside again.

He grinned. "I'm not sure anything short of hosing them down will help."

After nearly two hours spent scrubbing the kitchen, Noah emerged from the house and gazed with concern at his aunts. Slumped in the porch chairs, they stared sightlessly in front of them, deplete of energy. They'd come down from their sugar high with a crash.

"They'll be all right by this evening," Rhiannon said, flinging a thick wet strand of hair off her shoulder. "They've had showers and have changed into fresh dresses. All they need now is a nap."

He reached out and lightly touched her arm. "Thanks, honey. I appreciate all you've done."

Warmth tingled along her nerves at his tender endearment. He affected her—just like the sugar had affected Esme and Lavinia—intoxicating her, making her mindless and weak. She needed to get away from him and assess what was happening to her. "I should get back to the shop."

"I thought everything was closed today."

"Most businesses are, but I always make myself available during the afternoon. After yesterday's ball game, many of the costumes will need last-minute repairs." She bent and kissed Esme, then Lavinia. "Your pumpkins are going to be a big hit tonight."

"Thank you, dear," Esme said.

"Will you come by tonight?" Lavinia asked.

"Probably not, but I'll see you real soon."

"Don't move," Noah told his aunts. "I'll be right back." He drew Rhiannon off the porch and around the side of the house. "I hate to let you out of my sight," he said, a rueful grin on his face.

"The shop . . ."

"I know. And my aunts." He reached into his pocket and brought out a set of car keys. "Take my car back to town."

"Thanks." She hoped he didn't hear the relief in her voice, but she desperately wanted to be alone.

"I'll drive one of their cars in later."

"What do you mean?"

"You don't think I'm going to miss Halloween with you, do you? Not on your life."

He pressed a quick kiss to her lips. She shut her eyes, steeling herself against the inevitable surge of heat. He was always kissing her.

"I'll stay here with them and make sure they recover," he said. "I'll also contact my office and start the investigation rolling from that end. I should be able to make it to town by late this afternoon."

She nodded weakly. "Just in time for trick or treat."

He gathered her close. "What are you going to give me for a treat?"

She swallowed. "I told you. I'll be giving out cookies."

"That's for the kids. I'm talking about a special treat for me. Something on the order of last night. Although I don't see how anything could ever be that fabulous again. I'm willing to give it a try though. In fact, I'm willing to devote my whole life to the effort. How about you?"

She glanced away from him. "I've really got to go."

"Rhiannon? What is it, honey?"

"Nothing."

"Come on, Rhiannon. I remember you were starting to tell me something earlier."

She shook her head.

He frowned, dissatisfied. "I've got no choice except to let you go, but tonight, after everything is over, we'll talk. All right?"

"Take care of your aunts."

The afternoon sped by for Rhiannon. There were the expected repairs. A small fairy princess had beaten her brother over the head with her wand and broken it. Rhiannon supplied a glittering new one. A slightly larger Jason couldn't see out of his hockey mask. Adjustments were made. Casper's sheet had been dyed pink when his wife had accidently washed it with a pair of red sneakers. The sheet was replaced. One of the straps holding Igor's hump into place had to be tightened. And so it went.

Early celebrators stopped by to chat and discuss the chances that John Miller would take his ride tonight. Practically everyone asked after Noah.

The excitement built as the afternoon wore on, and Rhiannon allowed herself to be caught up in it. She loved the absurdity of Halloween—the way it brought out the child in the adults of Hilary, and the way it gifted such special memories to the children of the town, so different from the regimented atmosphere of the military bases she'd grown up on.

She'd only just managed to change into her

costume and get back downstairs when Noah arrived.

"Wow," he said, nearly speechless at her appearance.

Her costume was a floor-length black strapless dress with a long-sleeved bolero jacket that she'd created out of yards and yards of silk, lace, and net. Black sequins in the shape of moons and stars were strewn over the entire ensemble and glittered and sparkled with her every twist and turn.

She curtsied, coaxed to pleasure by his reaction. "I've always believed modern-day witches should be glamorous."

"You left out sexy," he added. "What spells are you going to cast tonight?"

"I don't cast spells," she said, very definite.

"Want to bet?" He chuckled. "My being here tonight instead of in New York City is living proof that you cast spells. And, as long as we're on the subject of spells"—he hesitated, unsure whether he really wanted to know the answer to the question he was about to ask—"what are all those weird-looking sticks and leaves that you keep in those glass jars?"

"Sticks and leaves?" Curious, she followed his gaze, then broke out laughing. "Haven't you ever seen potpourri before?"

"Po—what?"

She took one of the jars off the shelf, unscrewed the lid, and held it out to him. "It's a mixture of dried flowers, herbs, and spices. Mixing up different kinds of potpourri is sort of a hobby of mine." She saw the wary way he was staring into the jar. "This one has a cinnamon base. Nice for fall. Smell it."

He took a whiff. "You're right." He still needed explanations, he thought with amusement, but the acute relief he'd experienced at her answers over the last few days was gradually lessening and being replaced by an ordinary acceptance. He had certainly come far in just a few days.

She replaced the jar on the shelf. "How are Esme and Lavinia?"

"Just fine. They're back to their old selves. When I left, they were setting up for the evening out by the mailbox. They had their chairs there, plus all the pumpkin cakes they'd made. I thought all the action would be in town, but apparently they expect quite a few kids to come by."

"They'll get a lot of traffic, both in cars and on horseback."

"Good. I want the two of them of have a great time, because I sure plan to." He pulled her into his arms for a long, deep kiss that left her breathless and clinging. Only the sound of young voices calling "trick or treat" stopped him.

For the next few hours the town square was alive with ghosts and goblins, monsters and dragons. The gaiety infected Rhiannon, and along with Noah, she joined in the laughter and fun.

But in the back of her mind was the knowledge that she had a problem. Her reaction to Noah's lovemaking had knocked her completely off balance, leaving her feeling like a butterfly newly emerged from its cocoon, shatteringly vulnerable to the new sensations bombarding her.

"I'll close up now," she said. "I think most everyone's been by."

"Really?" He took a quick step outside and glanced around the mostly deserted square.

At his disappointed tone, her lips quirked. "It's late. Your aunts will be expecting you, won't they?"

He closed and locked the door. "I told them not to wait up for me, that I'd see them tomorrow."

Her heart began to pound with dread and excitement; her emotions were too confused to separate the two. "And how did they react to that?"

"As if I'd said I was driving to the store for a quart of milk. It's hard to say whether they're aware I'll be spending the night with you." He laughed. "I'd like to think they're not. Maybe they're just happy I'm staying in town a little longer."

Spending the night. The implication of the words panicked her. She turned and headed for the stairs, aware that he was right behind her.

She couldn't believe the quick and unquestioning way she had accepted her attraction for him. Hindsight was always twenty-twenty, and she supposed the unexpected passion she'd felt for Noah could excuse her. But now she was left to deal with the emotional consequences of that passion, and she wasn't sure she was up to the task.

Upstairs, she crossed into the bedroom, slipped out of her bolero, and tossed it on top of the screen.

Noah watched her, thinking that he hadn't meant to ignore the fact she was upset about something. His bubbling happiness simply refused to be suppressed, and he couldn't imagine anything being wrong. He felt some unseen hand had given him the world, and for a little while he'd forgotten that Rhiannon was no ordinary woman. But he remembered now.

"It's time, Rhiannon. If something's going on, I deserve to know what it is."

"You're right. I'm not being fair to you." She reached out for one of the brass chains that held up the bed and let the cool, solid metal support her. "There are some things I need to tell you. The problem is I'm not sure you're going to be able to understand. And I'm probably not going to be able to explain very well . . ."

"Try, Rhiannon."

Her teeth captured her bottom lip, worried with it, then released it. "Okay, here goes. I wasn't prepared for what happened last night. I thought I was . . . but I wasn't."

His brows came together. "What are you trying to say?"

"I'm not sure, and that's the point. As much as

I hate to admit this to you, I'm not sure about anything. I expected you to make love to me. I *wanted* you to. But suddenly everything is out of control." When she was growing up, the United States Navy had controlled her life, telling her father, and, therefore, telling her, when and where she had to move. The navy's power over her life had been a constant threat to her peace. She hadn't been able to do anything about that, but she could do something about this.

"Out of control," he said, repeating the words thoughtfully. "That's good. That means I'm not fighting this alone anymore."

She flung her hands out. "You're not fighting at all."

"And that upsets you?"

"You're overwhelming me." Her voice cracked. *Because what I feel for you scares me.*

"I thought I was loving you."

"Well don't!"

He jerked as if she'd hit him, and all the bubbles of happiness died inside him. "I think I understand. You found me amusing when I was a bumbling, stumbling idiot, so dazed by you and the mystique around you that I couldn't see straight. Is that it? You were playing with me like a cat batting at a ball of yarn?" He gave a sharp laugh. "That was sure as hell a bad metaphor. A normal cat bats at a ball of yarn. You and Graymalkin pursue more exotic amusements, don't you?"

"You're talking pure nonsense, Noah."

"Sorry, but I don't think so. You enjoyed seeing the super conservative, big-city lawyer out of his depth. You set out to get me, and with your spellbinding ways you had no doubts you'd do it. And now that you've succeeded, you're through with me. Okay. I think I've got everything straight now."

"No," she said, nearly crying. "None of what you've said is true."

"Oh? Then I can stay? And we can make love? And afterward plan our future together?"

"No." She'd never felt more miserable in her life.

"Right." The one word was heavy with disgust. He stared at her a minute, his hands on his hips. "If you think I'm going to thank you for the experience and drive meekly back to New York, you're wrong, lady. I'm not letting you get away with this without making you face what was and still is between us."

How ironic, she thought. He was telling her what until last night she'd been thinking about him. She'd wanted him to recognize and give in to the attraction between them. And now all she wanted to do was run from that very same attraction. She couldn't blame him, but knowing he was right and she was wrong didn't make his anger any easier to take.

"Look, Noah, I've done something really foolish here. In fact, I don't think in my whole life I've ever been this dumb about anything."

"I gather you're talking about our time in your bed last night." His voice was deadly quiet.

She wrung her hands together. "I have no excuses, and I can only apologize to you—"

"For *what*?" he exploded. "For driving me crazy until I had no alternative but to make love to you? Forget the apologies, lady. I'm not accepting them."

"You're going to have to, Noah, because right now that's all I can give you."

He reached out and jerked her against him. "You're wrong. I can make you give and give until you're too exhausted to do anything but lay on that bed and whimper for more."

She yanked violently away. *"Stop it."*

Everything went dark.

Her words echoed in the silence.

With a curse Noah turned his head toward the window. "The town's blacked out. Do you keep any matches and candles around here?"

She sighed. "I'll get them. I know the room better than you do." She made her way to the small table where she kept both matches and several candles.

Before the second candle was lit, Noah was behind her, taking the matches from her. "I'll light the rest."

Weary of arguing, she sat down on the bed, and after a few minutes, Noah was back.

He rested one knee on the bed and looked down

at her. "It doesn't pay to upset you, does it?" he said mildly.

"Noah, I had nothing to do with the lights. It's a rural area. Circuits get overloaded easily."

"Sure, sure."

"Dammit, stop patronizing me."

"Hey, I love reasonable explanations."

His sarcasm sent a shiver through her.

He leaned toward her. "I don't care if you made the lights go out or not. Feel free to make them go on and off as many times as you want. But it's not going to make me forget what's happened between us, and I won't let you forget either."

"Go, just go."

"I'll go, but first . . ." He pressed her back onto the bed.

"Noah, no—"

"I have to," he said roughly, shoving the black lace and silk out of his way. "I have to prove to myself that last night wasn't an aberration, that it wasn't just your magic working on me."

She didn't want this, she told herself. But even as she pushed weakly against his shoulders, she accepted and returned his searing kisses without being able to help herself. Heat wound through her, betraying her, then dominating every part of her body.

His hand went under her skirt, and he pushed the froth of black silk, net, and lace upward until his hand could smooth along her thigh to beneath the edge of her panties.

A cry broke from her lips, a cry of need, not of protest. Helpless tears seeped from beneath her lashes as she clutched at him, wanting him so.

Just a touch told Noah she was ready for him. He tore at his own clothing, then positioned himself between her legs and entered her. She gasped and arched up to meet him.

The black sequined stars and moons caught the candlelight, shimmering with every movement Rhiannon and Noah made. Together, they lost all control.

Rhiannon awoke to the sound of hoofbeats. Drawing the sheets around her, she rolled over and saw Noah, dressed and leaning against the wall beside the window.

"The power's back on," he said quietly, "and there's another teenager down there playing John Miller. Proof that nothing's real in this town."

Her stomach knotted at the bitterness in his voice. She knew it wasn't the nonappearance of John Miller's ghost he was angry about. But she was hurting, and at least for now she couldn't summon the energy or the courage to discuss it anymore. "John Miller may still come."

"How the hell would you know if he came or not? You said yourself you wouldn't look."

She exhaled slowly. "No, I wouldn't look."

"Right." He pushed away from the wall and glanced unseeingly around the room. "You know, your shop is aptly named. Illusions. Nothing is real. I thought I was touching you, but I was touching air." He paused, "I'm not going to apologize for what just happened between us."

She sat up and wrapped the sheet around her. "I don't recall asking you to."

He nodded. "And you don't have to ask me to leave either, because I'm going."

It felt as if her heart had turned to lead. "Where?"

"Does it matter?"

He took her silence for an answer.

Noah glanced at his watch, using the front porch light of Rhiannon's grandmother's house to see that it was two-thirty in the morning. It was lonely at this time of night with only his own thoughts for company, Noah concluded as he settled back among the pillows on the Victorian rattan sofa and covered himself with the blanket he'd taken from his car. He hadn't wanted to go back to his aunts' on the off chance they might hear him come in and want to talk, and he'd decided that this place was as good as any to sort through what had happened between Rhiannon and him. The sofa was comfortable; the blanket was warm. Now all he had to do was try to forget the aching hurt he felt and work out what he was going to do.

He knew now he'd made a bad mistake to force their lovemaking. She'd been like living fire in his arms, but he'd been dimly aware that the response was against her will. And afterward, he'd remained too bewildered and angry to try to reach out to her.

A movement at the corner of the porch caught his attention. He turned his head and saw Graymalkin. Noah wasn't surprised at this appearance. It had happened too many times before. But this time he knew Rhiannon hadn't sent the cat for him.

I'm not in the right place, am I? he silently asked Graymalkin, remembering how threatened the cat had been when he'd discovered something out of balance in his world.

Graymalkin's eyes gleamed eerily and pale blue as he stared at Noah for a long moment. Then he wheeled and trotted off, disappearing into the darkness.

Noah gazed after him. He had often compared Rhiannon and Graymalkin. Perhaps they were even more alike than he'd realized. Maybe more than she realized.

By watching Graymalkin over the past few days, he had learned that cats wanted to be where they were comfortable. They needed their own space, free to come and go at will. Like her pets, Rhiannon had lived a free and easy life-style in Hilary until he'd come along. Then they'd met and both of their worlds had been turned upside down.

Before they made love, he'd assumed their only

problem was his resistance to giving into her magical, mystical ways. He'd been wrong. Somehow he must have started making plans too fast and had come off too proprietary, leaving her feeling boxed in, frightened.

But wasn't that the normal response of a man in love? Normal. Ah, maybe that was the key. Rhiannon wasn't used to normal.

But he *was* normal.

Oh, hell, maybe he should just go back to New York.

Her self-possession had unnerved him from the first, along with the way she looked at him as if she knew exactly what he was feeling and found it amusing.

A sudden thought came to him. Her eyes had lost their serenity. Today there'd been no sign of her tranquility. Why?

He gazed into the darkness. The day they'd come out here, she'd said, "Just when I'd get comfortable, we'd have to move." She hadn't gone into detail, but he could see how a life whose only certainty was that you'd have to move again and again and leave behind your friends would be traumatic to a young girl.

She'd come to Hilary, the one stable environment she'd known, and created a province within which she could be what she wanted to be without causing anyone to so much as lift an eyebrow. There had been no danger that her life here would be disrupted.

Not until he'd come along. At first she hadn't been threatened. He had given her very little trouble, falling hard under her spell just as she'd wanted. But then she must have discovered that he, and the emotions he made her feel, didn't fit in her comfortable life.

Noah smiled. His reasoning made sense.

I'm beginning to understand you, Rhiannon, and if I ever completely figure you out, you won't have a chance.

His decision was made. He'd stay until he fit into her life. He'd act calm and unthreatening and give her time to study their situation from all sides until she became used to him and his love—just as Graymalkin had gradually become used to the chair.

There was another movement at the corner of the porch. Expecting Graymalkin, he turned and saw Rhiannon. Except for her pale hair and skin, she would have blended into the darkness.

She approached him warily, giving him the distinct impression that it would take only one wrong move on his part to make her bolt.

Briefly he wondered how she'd found him, then decided not to worry about it. For all he knew, Graymalkin could have led her to him. Or maybe she often came here when she needed to think. It didn't matter. He drew encouragement from the fact that however she'd found him, she had to be acting on some deeply buried need to be with him.

He forced himself to silence and stillness and was rewarded when she sat down beside him. He spread the blanket until it covered both of them, and she lay her head on his shoulder.

They didn't speak. In the distance an owl hooted. The hours passed. Together they watched the sun come up and tint the horizon with gently beautiful colors. And then Rhiannon left.

Seven

"What's wrong, dear?" Lavinia asked, gazing worriedly at Noah. "Don't you like roast beef?"

He started and glanced down at his plate. He'd been jabbing the roast beef sandwich with his fork, creating a neat line of holes across the middle of the bread. "No, I love roast beef." He'd slept until noon, refreshed himself with a shower and a change of clothes, but he couldn't seem to summon any interest in a late lunch. "The sandwich is really good. I guess I'm just not hungry."

Esme poured him a glass of iced tea. "Yesterday, when you told us not to wait up for you, we were hopeful things were going well."

Lavinia's lined face held a sad expression. "But it looks like we were wrong."

"What are you talking about?" Noah asked carefully.

"You and Rhiannon," the sisters said almost in chorus.

He pushed away his plate. "I appreciate your interest, but— "

"We *are* interested, and we want to know—"

"—how things are going," Esme said, finishing her sister's sentence and propping her elbows on the table.

"Yes, please tell us."

"Let's just say that for the rest of my stay I probably will be sleeping in your guest room."

The two sisters exchanged a concerned look.

"Oh, dear."

"That's a bad sign."

"For Rhiannon and me," Noah said, agreeing. "But I'll have more time to investigate the land buys around here. And now that Halloween is over, we'll be able to separate the strange and weird happenings that were done because of the holiday from the strange and weird happenings that are being done because someone wants your land."

Esme's tiny fist came down on the table. "I'd like to see anyone try to scare us away from our home."

"Our home," Lavinia echoed with a fierce nod of her head.

"The point is, someone may very well try to do just that," he said, "and if they do, I don't want you two here alone."

Esme reached over and patted his hand. "Don't worry about us. We don't scare that easily."

ave Daddy's sawed-off shotgun. Good for
g varmints and land grabbers."

Noah looked from one to the other, slightly perplexed. "You're not afraid?"

"Good heavens, no."

"Absolutely not."

"But I could have sworn your letter sounded worried."

"Oh, well . . ."

"We *were* worried."

"About you."

"Me?"

"Well, it's no secret that you work too hard. Your mother use to fret about it all the time."

"Not to mention disliking the women you were keeping company with."

"She was so afraid you'd marry one of them. None of us were exactly thrilled."

Noah stifled a groan. "You never even met any of the women I dated."

"Your mother told us about them."

"We knew once you came here and met Rhiannon, everything would be fine. You'd get married, settle down, stop working so hard, but—"

"—you never came to visit."

"So we decided to write and tell you about the little problem with the land."

"Little problem?"

"It's a problem," Esme acknowledged, "but it's not bothering us."

"Basically we're just curious."

Noah spent a full minute considering whether or not a jury of twelve sane men and women would convict him if he strangled his aunts. Or whether he cared if they did or not.

"So tell us, Noah—"

"What went wrong between you and Rhiannon?"

He pushed back from the table and stood up. "I'm going to make a phone call, then I'll be driving into town. Don't wait dinner for me."

After he left, Esme looked at her sister. "Do you think he seemed a little upset?"

"Nooo. What would he have to be upset about?"

Hilary seemed almost normal, Noah thought as he lingered over a cup of coffee in Blue's Diner. He used the word *almost* because an undercurrent of excitement persisted. It seemed no one had given up on John Miller's appearance, and somehow he wasn't surprised.

As he watched people come and go from the diner, he found it strange to see them without costumes. He'd become acquainted with Octopus-man, Godzilla, and Igor. Now he was going to have to learn their names all over again.

"How about a piece of apple pie?" Jeremiah Blue asked, standing beside Noah's booth. "My wife, Martha, made it fresh this morning."

Noah considered the prospect of a piece of pie with an open mind. He'd never in his life spent time doing absolutely nothing and consequently expert, but surely eating a piece of apple ... as good a way as any to kill time. "Why not," he said.

When Jeremiah brought him the pie, he topped off his coffee. "Glad to see you're still with us, Noah. I heard someone say you were planning on leaving before Halloween, but I knew that couldn't be right. No one in their right senses would want to miss Halloween."

Noah nodded. "That's the conclusion I came to."

"Enjoy the pie." Jeremiah slapped him on the back and started off. "Afternoon, Rhiannon."

Noah's head snapped up to see Rhiannon walking toward his booth.

"What can I get you, sweetie?" Jeremiah asked her as the two of them drew even.

"Nothing, thank you. May I join you, Noah?"

"Of course."

She slipped into the booth opposite him, pale, but composed. His effort to read the expression in her eyes was unsuccessful, but he viewed it a good sign that she had sought him out. He waited.

She regarded him from beneath her lashes, taking a moment to gather her courage. She'd known after they'd made love that she couldn't handle having him near, but after he'd stormed out of her house last night, she'd discovered she couldn't handle him *not* being near. She'd gone after him, driving around until she had spotted his car. The time with him on her grandmother's porch had been comforting, soothing, and exactly what she'd needed. But she understood it would be unrealistic to expect that sort of atmosphere to continue between them. There was too much passion between them. Too much pain.

What she had to discover was which hurt worse: having him or not having him.

She proceeded cautiously. "I thought you'd like to know, Clifford Montgomery is back."

The name clicked in his mind almost immediately. "The lawyer who sent out the letters outlining the offers for the land?"

"That's right."

"Good. I'll pay him a little visit."

She nodded. "I'll go with you."

Be careful, he told himself. "It's not necessary."

"You forget my grandmother's land is involved too. I don't want her coming home unless I know for sure she'll be safe."

"Fine. It would probably be better anyway to have someone there he knows and is comfortable with." He shoved the pie to the center of the table. "Have some."

She hesitated, then picked up his coffee spoon and helped herself to a small bite. "Thank you. I love Martha's apple pie."

"Esme and Lavinia surprised me this morning," he said casually, watching her eat. "They're not in the least worried or frightened about what's been going on and never have been. They're just curious."

Her brows arched in surprise. "But what about the letter they wrote you?"

"It turns out they had an ulterior motive. They wanted me to meet you."

"Oh." She laid the spoon down and sat back. "I didn't know."

"I didn't think you did. They're pretty crafty, those two."

She lowered her lashes over her eyes. "They'll be doubly disappointed when you return home."

"I'm sure they'll get over it. Shall we go see Mr. Montgomery?"

"Rhiannon, come in." A welcoming smile covered Clifford Montgomery's plump face as he showed her and Noah into his office. "Nice of you to drop by."

She returned his smile. "Thank you. Clifford, I'd like you to meet Noah Braxton."

"Why, you're Esme and Lavinia's nephew, aren't you?"

Noah hesitated, wondering if it would do any good to deny the relationship. In the end, he decided it wouldn't. "Yes, I am."

He grabbed Noah's hand and vigorously shook it. "It's a pleasure to meet you."

"How's your mother, Clifford?" Rhiannon asked.

"Much better, thank you. The flu bug really had hold of her there for a while, and I decided to spend an extra day, just to make sure she wouldn't have a relapse. I was real sorry to miss Halloween, though. How was it?"

"Great as always, although John Miller hasn't showed up yet."

The lawyer shook his head, *tsk*ing regretfully. "So I heard. It's such a shame. Everyone had high hopes this year."

"He could still come. He's been late before."

Clifford smiled at Noah. "Your aunts have told me all about you. Must be exciting to practice law in New York. Don't think I'd be up to it. Esme and Lavinia are quite proud of you, you know."

Rhiannon could tell by Noah's pained expression that his aunts weren't his favorite subject at the moment. "Clifford, Noah and I have come to see you on a business matter."

"Oh? Well, sit down, please, and tell me what I can do for you."

As they took the two leather chairs in front of the desk, Noah noted that Montgomery's office was extremely well appointed. Somehow, he'd expected something a bit more provincial. Outside the wide windows, two squirrels scampered over a wide lawn. Nice view, he thought before turning back to the lawyer. "I'd like to speak with you about the letter you sent my aunts regarding the offer on their land."

Clifford nodded. "Are they interested?"

"No, but they're curious as to who's behind the offer."

"Afraid I can't say. For now, at least, that's privileged information."

"Mr. Montgomery—"

"Call me Clifford."

He had become accustomed to the friendliness of the people of Hilary. Just as he had experienced culture shock his first couple of days there, he would experience a culture shock when he returned to New York. "Clifford, then. I don't understand how as a lawyer you can condone the things that have been going on. I'm certain the Virginia Bar Association would be interested to learn—"

His threat fell on deaf ears. Clifford had focused on an earlier part of his statement. "Condone? Condone what?"

Rhiannon spoke up. "Surely you know that the three people who have thus far agreed to sell their land were coerced."

As she outlined the events, Clifford's face gradually lost its color. "I assure you I have no knowledge of any of these incidents."

"Perhaps that's true," Noah said, "but we believe you client does have knowledge."

Clifford shifted nervously in his chair, but he didn't give in. "Knowledge is not guilt."

"No," Noah agreed, "but your client apparently has the motive. And motive leads to guilt. That's why we're asking you to tell us the name of your client."

Clifford's chin jutted slightly upward. "I'm sure you wouldn't betray a client's confidence, Noah. Why would you think I would?"

Noah was forced to reassess the man in front of him. Clifford Montgomery might be a small-town lawyer, but he was also ethically correct in not revealing the name of his client. "You're right. I wouldn't betray a client's confidence. But I strongly urge you to advise your client to reevaluate his plans. The properties of my aunts and Rhiannon's grandmother are involved, and I won't take kindly if anything, shall we say, unusual, happens to any of them or their land."

"I understand." Clifford stood somewhat jerkily. "Thank you for coming. The information you've given me has been most . . . interesting."

Noah rose and took the slightly damp palm Clifford offered. A minute later he and Rhiannon were walking away from the lawyer's office, and he was basking in the incredible day around them.

The brisk crystal air sharpened the senses, he thought with pleasure. The colors were so vivid they looked as if they'd been freshly mixed, and the scents were crisp and clean. If he were back at home, he'd be inside a concrete and steel skyscraper, accomplishing a great deal of work, but missing this beautiful day entirely. Mentally he weighed the day against the work and discovered to his surprise that the day came out ahead. But Rhiannon would have to be included in the day.

"What do you think about Clifford?" she asked.

"He stood his ground better than I expected, but he's worried. He'll definitely relay our message to his client. I'm doubtful, though, that it will do

any good. His client didn't let Clifford in on what
he had in mind because he obviously knew Clifford wouldn't approve."

"I agree, but what do we do now?"

As they approached her shop, their steps grew
slower. Her troubled gaze touched him, but he had
to be satisfied comforting her with only words.
"Don't worry about it. Mark, the man who I as-
signed to investigate the matter, will turn up something. In the meantime, your grandmother is
having a wonderful time with her sister, and I'm
here to protect my aunts."

She glanced away. "After last night I wasn't
sure. . . ."

"I told you I was going to stay as long as I could,
and nothing's changed that." A wry smiled tugged
as his mouth. "I hadn't realized what an interest
Esme and Lavinia had taken in my well-being. I
want to do everything I can to alleviate their
concern."

"Of course." Her tongue darted out to moisten
her bottom lip.

Witchcraft, he thought, and knew a sudden urge
to take her into his arms. The self-imposed lid
he'd put on his emotions was trying his strength.
Think of something mundane, he ordered himself. "Thanks for coming to tell me that Montgomery was back."

"Sure, no problem."

The autumn breeze played through her hair,
arranging the golden strands to its liking. He

watched and waited. If she wanted to get away from him, she would have to walk away first.

She slipped her hands into the pockets of the full black skirt she wore. "I *hate* this awkwardness between us."

Her outburst startled him. "I suppose that's what happens when two people stop being lovers," he said carefully.

"You suppose? Is that your experience?"

"Fishing, Rhiannon?"

She made a sound of frustration. "No."

"You're going to have to give me some guidelines here. I'm not sure what you want."

"I just think we should be able to find some sort of middle ground."

"You mean remain friends?"

Her head came up at his dubious tone. "Don't you think it would be possible?"

Going along with her on this would be the unthreatening thing to do, he thought, but he simply felt too strongly about the matter to lie. "I don't see it," he said grimly. "Not with you and me."

She shook her head, feeling helpless. "No, not with you and me."

She was silent for a minute, then suddenly she seemed to conjure a decisiveness out of nowhere.

"We should talk," she said.

"All right. When?"

"Now." She nodded her head toward the little park in the middle of the square. "Let's go over there."

"Fine."

They crossed the brick-paved street and strolled through the gold- and red-leaf-strewn grass to one of the park's benches. As soon as they were seated, she turned to him, and he could practically see her nerves.

"By now I'm sure you're convinced that I'm unhinged," she began.

He couldn't help smiling. "I think you're many things, but unhinged is not one of them."

With her palms up, she lightly laced her fingers together. "I wasn't able to explain before—at least not well—and I want to try again."

"I'm listening."

She nodded, vaguely annoyed by his self-possession. But she had asked for this talk, even though she wasn't entirely certain what she thought she could accomplish. "I've already told you that I wasn't prepared for what happened to me when you made love to me. I hadn't thought ahead. I hadn't realized there would be all these violent, explosive feelings and sensations."

Desire surged at her description of their lovemaking, and he had to dig deep for resources that would help him retain his composure. "That's understandable. You were a virgin. You'd never made love before."

"No, I hadn't. But I'm convinced that if I had made love with any other man, my first time would have been different. It's you, Noah. You made me feel those things. And afterward, it was worse."

She glanced down at her fingers, linked so tightly they had turned white. "Worse, in a different way. I was badly shaken by these crashing lows and euphoric highs I went through."   ·

His hopes rose: She'd just described love.

"I wasn't used to those feelings," she said, continuing. "And I definitely wasn't used to someone else having that much power over me."

He couldn't remain quiet any longer. "Don't you realize you have the same power over me?"

She watched a gust of wind send a small pile of leaves tumbling across the lawn. She laughed lightly without looking at him. "What I realize is that I must be terribly slow not to have known all of this beforehand."

He cupped his hand along her jaw and turned her to face him. "No. You created a life that made you happy. That's being smart. You sheltered yourself, but something new has come into your life— love—and your shelter's been removed.

She jerked away from him. "No. I'm sorry, but I'm not in love with you."

She spoke with such certainty, fear of losing her overcame his vow to be patient. "Why, Rhiannon? Because you've decided it wouldn't be comfortable or convenient to love me? Because I threaten your serenity?"

Rhiannon couldn't hold his gaze. She focused on the Victorian house across the street that had been the only real home she'd known in her life. It had been a place she'd been able to change and decorate exactly as she pleased, without worrying about putting holes in a navy-owned house, or damaging or altering too drastically a house her father had bought. Of necessity, they always had to be mindful of resale values.

Noah was very close to the truth, but she could go only so far in voicing her fears and worries. Her father had retired a commodore in the navy, and he had taught her military discipline at an early age. She'd learned never to cry or complain. And never to become too attached to someone, because in a relatively short time one of you would be moving on, and losing touch would be inevitable.

In this case, Noah would be the one to go. By saying he wanted to take her with him, he'd frightened her, and she was only now fully realizing why.

She loved this town and everyone in it. Although he'd become more relaxed about the eccentricities of Hilary, she couldn't see him ever becoming a part of the town. He could never live in Hilary. And she'd never leave. Hilary had given her the stability and love she'd always craved, and she couldn't give that security up.

Noah rubbed his hand over his face. Her silence was driving him crazy, and he could feel his resolve to be unthreatening about to come to an end. "Dammit, Rhiannon, talk to me. Scream at me, cast a spell, do something, but tell me what you're thinking."

"I'm thinking this isn't going to work. I thought talking things out might help, but I was wrong."

She stood so suddenly, he was taken off guard. He jerked to his feet and caught her shoulders in a firm grasp. "Dammit, I'm sorry I can't be a chair for you, but—"

"A what?"

"A chair. I can't let you just walk off like this, Rhiannon. In the long run I may not be able to change you mind, but, honey, I'm sure as hell going to give it a try."

She twisted within his hold, but he pulled her hard against him, stilling her. "No, Rhiannon. You're not going to get away from me. Work your witchcraft, make John Miller appear, create a storm in that clear blue sky above us, but I won't leave you alone until I've tried everything I can think of to make you realize that you love me."

"Noah—"

A car horn honked loudly at the edge of the park. They both looked around. Jerry Ornett, the mayor, was wildly waving and gesturing at them from the window of his car.

"We better go see what he wants," Rhiannon said, and with Noah beside her hurried over to the car.

"It's Graymalkin," Jerry told them. "He's on top of my roof, and he won't come down."

Rhiannon gave an exclamation of surprise. "Your roof? But there aren't any trees close to your house. How did he get up there?"

"He climbed up a ladder. The boys and I were demonstrating fire safety in two-story houses to the boy scout troop." The mayor switched his gaze to Noah and explained, "I'm the fire chief of our volunteer fire department."

Noah made a suitably impressed murmur. "How nice."

Rhiannon opened the back door of the car and slid in. Without a word Noah climbed in beside her.

The mayor's house, as Noah discovered a few minutes later, was a large two story with a steeply pitched roof. Twelve young boy scouts and seven volunteer firemen had their heads back, staring up at the roof.

Two more firemen were crawling on their bellies toward each other along the point of the roof. Graymalkin calmly sat between them, watching each man by turn. As soon as they got close enough to reach out for him, he slipped away to another position. This happened several times.

A few of the men and boys on the ground yelled out encouragement and suggestions. Others were too busy laughing.

"Here, kitty, kitty," one of the men closest to Noah called.

"I've tried that one before," Noah told him. "It won't work."

The man's face lit up as he saw who was speaking to him. "Hi, Noah. I'm Benjamin Geist. Remember?"

Noah slowly shook his head. "I'm sorry, but—"

"Octopusman."

"*Oh.* Hello. How are you?"

"Couldn't be better," Benjamin Geist said sincerely. "We've been having a great time this afternoon. Been teaching the boys fire safety and how to climb out of a second-story window and come down the ladder."

"I thought boys were born knowing that," Noah said with a grin.

"They need to be taught the *proper* way."

"Ah." Noah nodded understandingly.

"They also need to learn not to panic and to use their heads at all times. Things were going well, but then poor Graymalkin got stuck up there."

Poor Graymalkin? "Uh-uh." *Stuck?* That cat knew exactly what he was doing, Noah thought, glancing around. That's when he saw Merlin, sitting in a nearby tree, watching the proceedings. Something about the owl arrested his attention, and it took him a minute to figure out what it was. "That owl's actually laughing," he exclaimed, amazed.

Rhiannon and the mayor came up beside them just in time to hear him.

"Merlin would never laugh at Graymalkin," Rhiannon said to Noah. "He knows Graymalkin hates to be laughed at."

"You can see why we're concerned," Jerry said to both of them. "If we take the ladder away, Graymalkin will be stranded up there with no way down."

"On the other hand, if we leave the ladder where

it is and everyone goes away, the damned cat will get bored and come down by himself."

Shock registered on the faces of the mayor and Benjamin Geist. "We can't leave him up there," the mayor said.

"He might become confused, try to jump," Benjamin said.

"Even if he did, he'd be able to fly," Noah muttered.

Rhiannon watched Graymalkin as he adroitly outmaneuvered another fireman who had joined the two on the roof. "He's playing games up there."

Jerry smiled affectionately. "He's a fun-loving little thing, isn't he?" He cupped his hands around his mouth and yelled to one of the men on the roof. "John, see if you can circle around behind him."

John sent Jerry a look that mixed incredulity with horror.

Noah walked to the middle of the yard. From his current position on the roof beside the chimney, Graymalkin followed Noah's progress.

"Graymalkin," Noah said in a calm but firm tone, "come down."

As if he'd been waiting for Noah's command, the cat stood, skillfully made his way to the edge of the roof, and walked headfirst down the ladder. When he was halfway down, he slowed and placed all four feet on the same rung. Then with a gathering of muscle and black fur, he leapt to Noah.

Noah stared bemusedly at the black cat in his

arms. He'd expected him to come down off the roof. But never in a million years would he have anticipated that he would jump to him.

Rhiannon came up beside them. "Graymalkin likes you."

"What this damn cat likes," Noah said, "is to harass me." He dumped the cat to the ground. When he looked back at Rhiannon, he saw the familiar twinkle had returned to her eyes. Immediately his annoyance faded.

"He's not harassing you, Noah. He likes you, but he knows you don't like him."

"And that's why he's been haunting me?"

"Exactly. He's been letting you get used to him slowly."

He stared at her. "That doesn't even come close to a reasonable explanation. You're talking as if he has a degree in psychology."

She shrugged. "I'm telling you, he likes you."

Graymalkin trotted over to the group of boy scouts and allowed them to pet him.

Jerry came up to Noah and Rhiannon. "Well, now that the excitement's all over, would you two like to stay and see the rest of the demonstration?"

Without looking at Noah, Rhiannon said, "If you don't mind, Jerry, I think we should be getting back to the shop."

"Sure, sure, no problem. Benjamin can run you over there."

"By the way," she said. "You might want to wind up the demonstration and get the boys home early so they can do their chores. We're in for a storm this evening."

Both the mayor and Noah glanced up at the cloudless sky.

"I'll do that," Jerry said. "Thanks for telling me."

"A storm, Rhiannon?" Noah asked.

"Yes."

"Are you ready?" Benjamin called, already at his car.

She nodded, then paused to give Graymalkin and Merlin a look. Merlin lifted his wings and took flight in the direction of her house. Graymalkin left the boy scouts without a backward glance and took off running in the same direction.

Rhiannon gently grasped Noah's hand in hers and led him to the car.

Eight

The storm broke just as Rhiannon and Noah were finishing dinner. He'd suggested that they stop by Blue's Diner and buy something to take to her house and eat. It had been an obvious ploy to spend more time with her, and he'd been slightly surprised when she'd agreed. Jeremiah Blue had happily dished up two orders of Brunswick stew for them, added a loaf of homemade bread to their order, and at the last minute insisted they take a hefty portion of rice pudding.

Now, as thunder boomed overhead, Noah pushed away the half-eaten dish of pudding and gazed at Rhiannon with an expression of sincere interest. "I've never experienced a storm conjured up by a witch before. Just how intense will it be?"

She sighed. "I didn't conjure up the storm. I simply said we would have one this evening."

"Rhiannon, there's never been a clearer sky than the one we had today."

She shrugged. "There were signs."

"Uh-huh. Signs obviously not visible to the average person."

She leaned back in the chair and folded her hands across her waist. "I suppose you want an explanation."

"It would be nice."

"It would also be easy. You see, I'm the daughter of a career navy officer. Weather is very important to men who spend a great deal of their life at sea. My father taught me to read a sky almost before I could read a book."

"Okay," he said, his tone calm.

She seemed to him more witchlike than ever as she tilted her head to one side and regarded him out of her almond-shaped eyes.

"Do you believe me?"

"It's a great explanation."

"Thank you. I know how important explanations are to you, so I try to have good ones." With that, she flashed him a breathtaking grin and stood. "Since you bought dinner, I'll do the dishes."

She found herself humming as she cleared the table and took their plates and cutlery into the kitchen. In the midst of her turmoil, there had been the relative calm of this special interlude, and it had been wonderful. For a while the disturbed state of her mind had stilled, allowing her to feel warm and content. But she knew the feeling wouldn't last. She had a decision to make that would affect her whole life. For both Noah and herself, she had to make the decision soon.

This afternoon, with a crowd of people waiting to see what he would do, Graymalkin had chosen to leap to Noah. She'd envied Graymalkin his certainty.

"Where's Graymalkin?" he asked.

She paused, teasing glints sparkling in her eyes. "Do you miss him?"

"It's more a case that I feel safer when I know where he is and what he's up to," he said dryly.

"I think you like him."

"You've got to be kidding. He's nothing but a *damned* nuisance." Thunder cracked, rattling the windowpanes. He looked at the window, then back at her. "Sorry, I didn't mean to upset you."

With a laugh she picked up a dishtowel and threw it at him. "I still think you like Graymalkin, and the last I saw him, he was downstairs on his pillow."

"Ah, yes, the blue satin pillow on top of the curio cabinet. I remember the pillow well. The blue satin matched his collar, which matched his eyes—which matched your eyes."

"He likes it down in the shop."

"That makes sense. With all those ghosts and gremlins down there, he probably feels right at home."

"I still think you like him."

He grinned, enjoying their banter. "Whatever you say."

Her expression suddenly changed to one of concern as she gazed over his shoulder. "The storm is upsetting Merlin. I'd better take him downstairs."

He glanced at the owl who, as usual, was perched atop the armoire. The owl didn't appear upset to him. But then, he had no idea what an upset owl would look like. How did she, he wondered.

"Merlin," she said softly.

The owl flew to her shoulder.

Noah frowned at the woman and bird. "Why would a storm frighten him? If he wasn't your pet, he'd be out in it."

"But he is my pet and storms do upset him." She gave the owl a sweet, reassuring smile. "I'm going to take him downstairs, where there aren't as many windows. He'll feel more secure there. I won't be long."

Noah brooded while she was gone. He knew what he had to do when she returned. He had to act like a polite guest who'd come for dinner and now knew it was time to leave. Except . . . how could he? For the life of him, he couldn't consider himself just a guest. They'd made love—and he'd fallen in love with her—and the thought of being without her tonight was like a knife straight through his heart.

He knew her doubts and uncertainties still stood between them, but despite his vow to be unthreatening, his patience was ebbing and flowing like the tide, and if he wasn't careful, he could ruin everything.

They'd had a nice day together. They'd talked and laughed. All in all, he felt they had made real progress. And, oh, hell. He had to leave.

When she returned she set about the task of tidying up the small kitchen with quickness and efficiency.

"Are you sure I can't help you?" he asked.

"I'm sure. There's not much to be done."

He watched her, the hurting in him intensifying by degrees as the minutes passed, too quickly. Finally he tore his gaze away from her. "I should be going," he murmured, and rose.

She paused in the act of folding a dishtowel. This was the moment she'd been dreading. *She didn't want him to leave, but she couldn't let him stay.*

"Yes," she said. "The storm may worsen, and you don't want to be out in it when that happens."

"No, I guess not." He glanced around the loft. She'd lit several candles as a preventive measure against the possibility of another power outage. "Are you going to be all right here?"

"You mean because of the storm? I'll be fine. It's you I'm worried about. You've got to drive in it."

There was only one thought in his head: walking out the door. That's why it came as such a shock to him when he said, "Maybe I should reconsider leaving. I mean, it's been raining so hard, the roads could already have turned treacherous."

He'd never said exactly when he planned to go back to New York, she realized, and there was a possibility she wouldn't see him again after tonight.

"The car could slide right off the road and get stuck in a ditch." He couldn't believe what he was doing. He'd simply started talking, and now he couldn't seem to stop. "Then when I opened the door and climbed out, my shoes would sink right down into the mud. When I tried to pull my shoes out, the shoes would stay in the mud, and I'd be left with only my socks on my feet."

Rhiannon stared at him. *What was he saying?*

"I'd have to try to walk to my aunts in my socks. That road's not well traveled, but if someone did happen by, they wouldn't stop—not for a demented man walking in the rain without any shoes."

Tears welled in her eyes, and she smiled. He really was adorable . . . even if he was a big-city lawyer who couldn't get use to Hilary and made her feel vulnerable, depressed, and wildly excited.

"The people would probably drive by so fast, their car would spray even more water over me— muddy water." He felt like a babbling idiot, but at least she was listening to him. "When I got home, Esme and Lavinia would force me to drink hot tea and take nasty medicine. They'd probably even put a mustard plaster on my chest, wrap a red wool sock around my neck, and fasten it with a huge safety pin."

What should she do, she wondered. For the first time in her life, she found she couldn't depend on her instincts. They were sending her mixed signals.

"Esme and Lavinia would insist on making me

chicken soup, but because they wouldn't have any chicken in the freezer, they'd have to tramp out to barn in the rain, getting soaking wet in the process." Why didn't she say something? Do something? Tell him to shut up. Tell him to go. Tell him to stay. "They'd spy some unsuspecting chicken who had already settled down for the night. There he'd be, nice and warm with his feathers all fluffy, and they'd grab him up and do the poor thing in."

She wanted to laugh. She wanted to cry.

"And all three of us would end up in bed sick with pneumonia with no one to take care of us."

He really was funny. She really was sad.

"That might happen, Rhiannon." He took a deep, calming breath. "Or you could let me stay here with you, and I could hold you all night long."

Tears slipped from her eyes and spilled down her cheeks.

"Oh, no . . ." With a groan he went to her and took her into his arms. "Don't cry, honey. I didn't mean to upset you."

"You didn't," she murmured, her face pressed against his chest.

"Then what's wrong?"

"It's just that you're so silly."

"*Foolish* is another good word to describe me, and the funny thing is that I've never been either silly or foolish before." He pulled away and gazed down at her. "Rhiannon, may I stay with you tonight. I really do want just to hold you . . . and I want it more than anything in the world."

"Yes," she whispered. "Please stay. Hold me."

They lay down together on a bed suspended by four golden chains and fell asleep to the sound of rain. And he held her all night long.

Noah heard the phone ringing. Beside him, Rhiannon stirred. He parted his eyes to a slit, lifted his head, and searched the room until he spotted the phone. "Do you want me to get it?"

"The phone's over there," Rhiannon said without opening her eyes or indicating where she meant.

"Thanks," he said wryly, and concentrated on reaching the phone without stumbling over anything. "Hello."

"Noah? This is Mark."

"Mark? How did you find me?"

"I called your aunts, and they gave me this number."

"Great," he muttered, disgusted, but not surprised that Esme and Lavinia had been so sure they knew where he was.

"I'm sorry if I woke you up, but it's ten o'clock and—"

"Ten? It can't be. I've never slept that late in my life."

"Well, you did this morning."

Noah glanced out the window. Astonishingly, all traces of the storm had disappeared, and the sun was shining brightly. "Don't worry about waking me. Have you found anything?"

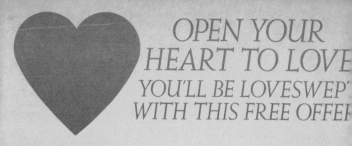

OPEN YOUR HEART TO LOVE
YOU'LL BE LOVESWEPT WITH THIS FREE OFFER

HERE'S WHAT YOU GET:

1. **FREE! SIX NEW LOVESWEPT NOVELS!** You get 6 beautiful stories filled with passion, romance, laughter, and tears... exciting romances to stir the excitement of falling in love... again and again.

2. **FREE! A BEAUTIFUL MAKEUP CASE WITH A MIRROR THAT LIGHTS UP!**
What could be more useful than a makeup case with a mirror that lights up*? Once you open the tortoise-shell finish case, you have a choice of brushes... for your lips, your eyes, and your blushing cheeks.

*(batteries not included)

3. **SAVE! MONEY-SAVING HOME DELIVERY!** Join the Loveswept at-home reader service and we'll send you 6 new novels each month. You always get 15 days to preview them before you decide. Each book is yours for only $2.09 — a savings of 41¢ per book.

4. **BEAT THE CROWDS!** You'll always receive your Loveswept books before they are available in bookstores. You'll be the first to thrill to these exciting new stories.

BE LOVESWEPT TODAY — JUST COMPLETE, DETACH AND MAIL YOUR FREE-OFFER CARD.

FREE-LIGHTED MAKEUP CASE!
FREE-6 LOVESWEPT NOVELS!

- NO OBLIGATION
- NO PURCHASE NECESSARY

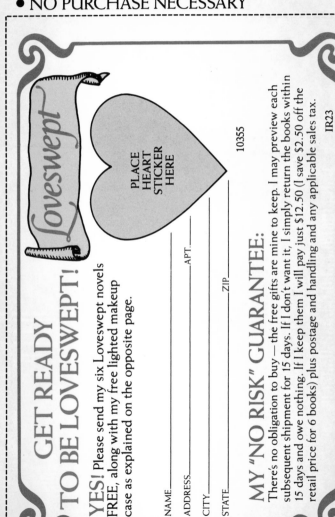

REMEMBER!

- The free books and gift are mine to keep!
- There is no obligation!
- I may preview each shipment for 15 days!
- I can cancel anytime!

(DETACH AND MAIL CARD TODAY.)

BUSINESS REPLY MAIL
FIRST-CLASS MAIL   PERMIT NO. 2456   HICKSVILLE, N.Y.

POSTAGE WILL BE PAID BY ADDRESSEE

Loveswept

Bantam Books
P.O. Box 985
Hicksville, NY 11802-9827

"Sure have. I had a damn hard time, and I owe about a dozen favors, but I finally found a company from Upstate New York by the name of Collin Chemicals who is interested in relocating their plant. Have you heard of them?"

"I don't think so."

"They're a solid company with several new contracts and unlimited growth potential. Thus the relocation plans."

"And they've decided on Hilary?"

"It doesn't seem to be definite just yet. They've investigated several alternate sites, but as near as I can determine, they're leaning toward Hilary. It's hard to say precisely what they're up to, though. Collin Chemicals plays their cards close to the vest, and they're so discreet, they positively whisper."

"That must be why no one in Hilary has heard anything about it."

"You're wrong. I know for sure they've spoken to the mayor, a Jerry Ornett. And at least one other person is *very* well informed. I managed to get hold of the company's telephone records and found quite a few calls to Hilary."

Noah tensed. "And?"

"The person being called is named, just a minute, let me check my notes . . . his name is Martin Richardson. Know him?"

"Martin Richardson? That name sounds familiar." He rubbed his face, trying to clear the remaining sleep from his head, then he glanced at Rhiannon, who was sitting up in bed, her arms around her drawn up knees, watching him. "Who's Martin Richardson?" he asked her.

"He's the real estate agent you spoke with the night of the carnival. Dracula."

"Dracula. Right. Mark? Yes, I know him."

"Noah, did you say Dracula?"

"Never mind. Have you found out anything else?"

"I haven't discovered who Richardson's contact is in the company, but I do know that a William Stratford is Collin's man in charge of the relocation. According to my sources, he's ready to make his final decision, and he'll be in Hilary today."

Noah nodded. "That could be a valuable piece of information. Mark, you've done an excellent job."

"Thanks. Anything else I can do?"

"I'll get back in touch with you if I can think of anything. Thank you for your help. Good-bye." Noah hung up the phone and turned toward Rhiannon.

She slid off the bed and brushed at the wrinkles in her black skirt. Both of them had slept in their clothes. "What's up?"

"I need to speak with Martin and the mayor."

"Jerry?"

He briefly explained Mark's end of the conversation.

"It's hard for me to believe that either Jerry or Martin are involved in this," she said.

"I know. It's hard for me too." He paused for a moment, frowning as he realized he liked both men. Odd. It usually took him a long time to warm up to a person. "Let's don't jump to any conclusions yet. We won't know anything for sure until I talk with them." He glanced down at himself. "First, though, I need to clean up a bit."

"Me too. Would you wait while I shower and change? Afterward I could ride with you to Esme and Lavinia's while you do the same. Then we could both go talk with Jerry and Martin."

He stared at her, remembering the joy he'd known, holding her through the night. "I'll wait for you," he said.

What was she doing here with Noah, Rhiannon wondered, sitting beside him as they drove back from Esme and Lavinia's. Despite her serious reservations that a relationship between them could work, she was taking every opportunity to be with him.

With the sure knowledge that she should say no, she'd said yes to his idea for dinner last night, and she'd had a relaxing, enjoyable time.

She'd said yes when he'd asked if he could spend the night, and for a while she'd known peace in the middle of a storm.

This morning she hadn't been able to let him leave without her, and she'd insisted on coming with him. And instead of pondering what would happen when they spoke with Jerry and Martin, here she was thinking of the man sitting beside her.

He'd showered and changed clothes, topping

coffee-brown trousers and a lighter brown sports shirt with a brown plaid camel hair jacket. He accused her of witchcraft, of casting a spell over him. The truth was, she was as caught up in the spell as he was.

She shut her eyes. What was her problem? She'd never known a nicer, more desirable man than Noah. And he'd never deliberately hurt her. But because of him, she was hurting. She glanced over at him. He appeared relaxed and confident as he sat behind the wheel, concentrating on the drive. Was it possible he was hurting as she was?

He'd made it plain that he wanted her with him, but his life was a world away from Hilary. He wouldn't allow himself to be swept up in the lunacies of this town and her life because he knew he didn't belong or fit. But this was the only place on earth where she did fit.

Maybe there was no real decision to be made, she thought sadly. Maybe her brief time with Noah would have to be a precious memory and nothing more.

She suddenly heard him give an exclamation. "There's the mayor." He honked the horn and turned the car into the first available parking space.

Jerry had been strolling along the sidewalk, but when he saw who was honking at him, he stopped to wait for them, a big smile on his face. "Hi, Noah, Rhiannon. What are you two up to today?"

"We were loooking for you," she said.

"Oh? What can I do for you?"

"We've heard," Noah said, "that Collin Chemicals has been in contact with you regarding the possibility of relocating their plant and their people here."

The mayor nodded, polite and helpful. "That's right."

Noah couldn't quite believe Jerry had answered so easily. "Why didn't you tell me this?"

"Why should I tell you something like that?" Jerry asked, genuinely bewildered.

"Do you remember letting me into the courthouse the day of the ball game? I said I was interested in the land on the east side of town and I wanted to check some of the records?"

"Sure. You said you were interested in the investment possibilities. But, Noah, you never mentioned the Collin Chemical company relocation."

"No, because I didn't think you'd tell me what I wanted to know."

"Well, why in the world not?"

"You mean you *would* have?"

"Of course." Jerry glanced at Rhiannon, then back at Noah. "I don't understand. What's wrong?"

Noah exhaled a long breath of air, rearranging his thoughts. "We're not sure. How many other people know about Collin Chemicals? I mean, did you announce that they had contacted you?"

"No." He shrugged. "They made only an unofficial inquiry. We've gotten similar nibbles over the years, but nothing's ever come from it. Do you know these people, Noah?"

"No," he said, his voice grim, "I haven't had that pleasure yet. Thanks, Jerry. I may be getting back to you on this. In the meantime, Rhiannon and I have someone else to see."

They found Martin Richardson alone in his real estate office. When he heard the door open, he looked up with a smile. But the smile quickly changed to one of stunned surprise when he saw Noah. "Hello, there. I thought you'd planned on heading back up north after Halloween."

"My plans changed."

His expression cleared as he took in who was with Noah. "I *see*. Well, congratulations, you two." He stood and extended his hand. "I couldn't be happier, and I know Esme and Lav—"

"We didn't come here to talk about ourselves, Martin," Rhiannon said, interrupting.

"Oh?" His hand slowly dropped back to his side.

Noah pushed his sport coat back and slipped his hands into the pockets of his slacks. "When my aunts told me the strange things that had happened to three of the landowners who live east of here, along with the high offer they'd received for their land, I started an investigation of the situation. So far I've discovered that a New York company called Collin Chemicals is interested in relocating to Hilary, and that someone with that company has been calling you here at this number. The next thing I intend to find out is why."

Martin had grown pale, and he dropped into his chair. "I, uh, answered a few questions for them regarding the availability of land in this area. You know, normal real estate questions, that sort of thing."

"Martin," Rhiannon said gently, "I've known you for a long time, and you've never lied."

"I know," he said wearily, sinking farther back into his chair. "I'm just not any good at it. My mother always told me you should leave what you aren't good at to other people."

Noah placed the flat of his hands on the top of the desk and leaned toward him. "Did you leave the task of scaring three landowners off their land to someone else, Martin, or was that something you were good at?"

He wiped his hand across his forehead. "I never wanted to hurt anyone. I hope you two believe that. In fact, I was uneasy about the whole deal, right from the start. I told Arthur I wouldn't be any good at this."

"You told who?" Rhiannon asked.

"Arthur Holden. He and I went to school together at William and Mary, and we've stayed in touch through the years." With a look at Noah, he grimaced. "He works for Collin Chemicals."

Noah nodded. "And when he heard they were interested in Hilary, he decided it would be a golden opportunity for the two of you to make some money."

"A *lot* of money. Still, I told him I wouldn't cheat my friends."

Rhiannon folded her arms across her chest. "That was awfully nice of you, Martin."

He winced at her sarcasm.

"And also, completely unethical."

"I offered everyone, including your grandmother, a price that was way over market. No one would have given them what I was prepared to give."

"Except Collin Chemicals," Noah said, "and they would have given them twice that amount. Right?"

Rhiannon's hands clenched at her side. "That is, Collin would have *if* the landowners had wanted to sell, which they didn't, which was why you resorted to scare tactics. Martin, how could you?"

"Aw, hell, Rhiannon, I don't know." He picked up a pencil and tossed it across the room. "Like I said, Arthur talked me into it, and I didn't figure there'd be any harm in trying."

Noah shook his head, half disgusted, half amused. Martin was acting exactly like a little boy who'd been caught playing hooky. "The thing of it is, harm has been done, and as a result, you, Martin, are going to help us put things right."

"But how?"

"I'm not sure." Noah looked at Rhiannon. "Mark said that William Stratford, the man who is the head of Collin's relocation, will be in town today. It looks like a final decision is imminent."

"The question is, then, what is going to be best for the town."

"Right. And to find that out I suggest we call an impromptu town meeting."

Her eyes began to twinkle. "At Blue's Diner?"

He grinned. "You're reading my mind, honey." He turned back to Martin. "You'll come with us."

"Noah, you're not going to tell everyone how I'm involved in this, are you?"

He paused. "I'm going to wait and see what needs to be done. But you can forget your profits. Escrow hasn't closed, and you're backing out of the deal as of this minute. Tell Clifford Montgomery to start on it immediately. Oh, and the three landowners will keep the money you advanced them."

"*Noah.*"

"Martin," Rhiannon said in a warning voice, "you're not the injured party in this shady deal, and I strongly suggest you stop acting like you are."

Nine

Noah gazed around Blue's Diner. People stood shoulder to shoulder, intent on the discussion taking place. Listening to them talk, Noah found it hard to remain an objective observer, because he understood, now, how important Hilary and its life-style was to these people. He also understood why they weren't sure what to do.

Esme and Lavinia were currently holding forth.

Esme shook her pink-and-strawberry-haired head for emphasis. "We don't want to see Hilary changed, and we won't sell Collin Chemicals our land."

"But we won't stand in the town's way if it's what you decide you want," Lavinia said.

"We want to live this last part of our lives in our own home," Esme said.

Lavinia gestured to Noah. "But after we're gone, if Noah wants to sell our land to them, he can."

"The point is," Jeremiah Blue said, "can we really stop them if they choose Hilary?"

Everyone looked at Noah expectantly, and after a brief hesitation he decided that he wasn't helping matters by remaining quiet. "You could annex the land they're interested in and refuse to rezone it for business. And if that wasn't feasible, then you could make it unattractive and economically difficult for Collin to meet your requirements concerning roads and other infrastructure for their development."

"That's good," Esme said with approval.

Noah gazed around the room, trying to gauge if those assembled truly understood the enormity of what could happen. "There's something else you need to think about. Collin would need access into the city water supply and electricity. That would entail expanding your current system. To do that would cost a great deal of money."

Lavinia clucked her tongue. "Uh-oh. That's bad."

"But it would also eventually generate tremendous revenue for the city."

"That's good," Martha Blue said, pausing in the act of pouring out coffee. Then she added, "I suppose."

"There would also be increased tax revenues," Noah said.

Jerry Ornett held up a fork piled high with

apple pie. "Wait a minute. We're not exactly hurting now. We have everything we need."

Everyone in the diner nodded in agreement.

Noah continued. "You would no longer have to have fund-raising carnivals to obtain money for things like new high school band uniforms. The money would be there for you."

"No more carnivals?" Louella Gibson, the town's other real estate agent, asked with dismay.

Noah rubbed his eyes with his thumb and forefinger. He shouldn't have mentioned the carnival. "But there would be new jobs for you and your children. You wouldn't lose your young people to bigger towns. When they grow up, employment would be available for them."

"There's always been enough jobs to go around," Christopher Dean, the man who owned the bakery, said.

Jerry waved his now-empty fork and spoke with a full mouth. "And our kids like it here. Not many of them leave, but those who do usually go only as far as Richmond."

"And they always come back," Louella Gibson said. "Especially for Halloween."

"I suppose a few new jobs would be nice," Margery McConnell, the church secretary, said tentatively.

Noah shook his head. "I don't think you people understand what we're talking about here. There would be more than a *few* new jobs. If Collin Chemicals relocates, they'd build a huge plant, and bring in hundreds of people who are already in their employ to work in that plant. To meet the needs of those new people, there would have to be whole developments of houses, more grocery stores, larger and better medical facilities, new schools, and shopping malls, just to name the obvious, and all of those facilities would have to be built, stocked, and manned."

A shocked silence fell over the group.

Finally Jerry spoke up. "You're talking about making Hilary a whole new town."

"Just about," Noah agreed.

"If this goes through, is there any way we could protect ourselves?" Rhiannon asked. "Could we make sure that our way of life isn't ruined and that the things we feel are important remain the same?"

It was the first time Rhiannon had spoken. Beneath the calmly asked question, he could detect real distress, and he answered carefully. "The sheer size of the company and the number of its people would dictate that you could do only so much. That's the downside. The upside is that the Collin relocation would be a tremendous boon to the economy, and I do emphasize the word *tremendous.*"

Jeremiah Blue gazed thoughtfully at Noah. "It sounds like you think we should welcome these people with open arms."

Noah held up his hands. "I'm not recommending anything. I'm just trying to point out to you both the benefits and the drawbacks of the deal."

"But what would you recommend?" a matronly lady asked. She was standing next to the baker and wearing a flour-covered apron.

Rhiannon held her breath, waiting to see what he would say. All along, Noah had held himself aloof from the town, but this would be the perfect opportunity for him to become involved. If he would only make some sort of emotional commitment to the place she loved so dearly, maybe . . .

"It's not up to me to recommend anything. You people are the ones who are going to have to live with whatever decision you make."

Cold disappointment spread through her at his answer.

"Well, we have to decide something," Judy Mercer, the local innkeeper, said. "That man from Collin is over at the inn right now, waiting for Martin."

Martin Richardson shifted uncomfortably beneath the stares. "I'm supposed to drive him out to the proposed site this afternoon. We're to look at all the properties involved."

Noah scanned the diner, taking in the worried expressions of the people gathered there. His gaze lit last on Rhiannon. He thought he caught a hint of a challenge in her eyes, and although he wasn't sure what it meant, he knew what he was feeling. "Look, people, I get the distinct impression you're not too keen on this."

"Hilary was invaded once before by Yankees," someone standing near the back grumbled. "We didn't like it then; we don't like it now."

Jerry rubbed his neck. "I'm not sure what to do. The thing is, how can we turn away an opportunity for a chance to improve the town?"

"I'm not sure it would be an improvement," Jeremiah said.

Rhiannon waited until everyone had voiced their agreement with Jeremiah, then she said, "I don't think any of us want to see Hilary changed as much as this company would change us. The question is, would they accept a no from us? I mean, how much pressure would they bring to bear on us?"

Surprisingly it was Martin who spoke up. "I've learned a few things about Collin, and you should know they have a lot of money and legal power behind them. If they choose Hilary, and the last I heard it's practically a certainty, they'll throw everything they have into convincing us to let them move here. I, uh, I've heard there'll be incentive packages that we won't be able to refuse."

A chorus of groans followed his statement.

"Do you know how they feel about Halloween, Martin?" Lavinia asked.

Martin shook his head.

"I don't think we can count on them viewing it the same way as we do," Jerry said glumly.

"That tears it," Jeremiah said.

"What are we going to do?" the shoemaker asked.

Noah absorbed their dismay and unhappiness, and he didn't need to look at Rhiannon to know that she shared their feeling. Suddenly, doing something to help them seemed the most natural thing in the world. "I have an idea," he said quietly.

Rhiannon glanced at him with amazement. "What is it?"

"I'd rather not say at the moment. It might not even work. Martin, arrange your schedule with William Stratford so that you and he are out at Rhiannon's grandmother's place at dusk in the big field west of the house."

Martin made a reluctant face but nodded his agreement.

"Rhiannon, I'd like you to be there too. Locate a spot where you can see the field but Stratford can't see you."

"All right. There's the hayloft of the barn, but—"

"No questions." His gentle smile was meant to take the sting out of his abrupt words. Then he turned to the rest of the people. "Everyone else go about your normal business. But tomorrow, wear your Halloween costumes. I want to make sure William Stratford gets a real good idea of what this town is like."

Rhiannon took a seat on the floor of the hayloft by the open doors and leaned back against a bale of hay. Below and beyond, she had an uninterrupted view of the field. Night was approaching, but she could see Martin and William Stratford. Their conversation rose through the still air to her, complete and intact. Noah was nowhere in sight.

She plucked a piece of hay from the bale and chewed on it. The town had taken their assignment from him very seriously, and there'd been a steady stream of people into the shop all day, renting or buying costumes, or discussing ideas for renovating old ones and even for making new ones. The town viewed the opportunity to wear costumes tomorrow as a "bonus" of sorts and planned to go all out. She'd been kept busy, but Noah had never been far from her thoughts. Where was he, she wondered, and what was he up to.

Below her, William Stratford fixed a stern gaze on Martin. "One of our executives, Arthur Holden, let drop that you and he own three of the properties we'll need to acquire. Is this one of them?"

"Uh, no. In fact, Arthur and I don't own any of the land you want. Those deals never went through, but, uh, Arthur doesn't know about it yet."

"I see. Well, I'm relieved to hear it. Our company wants no hint of a scandal, and if one of our employees was using inside information on this relocation to make a profit, it would look very bad for us. We couldn't allow it, you understand. I had planned to look over the situation here, then return and speak with Arthur."

"There's no need to worry about it any longer, Mr. Stratford."

"You're sure?"

"Unfortunately, I'm positive."

"That's good." Stratford slapped him on the back. "It's getting dark. I guess it's time we were returning to town."

"Uh, if you don't mind, I'd like to stay out here a little longer. I want to see . . . uh . . . well, just a little longer."

Stratford cast him an odd look, but shrugged. "All right, then. Martin, one of the reasons I contacted you to show me around was because Arthur told me you've lived in Hilary your whole life. Now, I've studied the land and have come to the conclusion that it's perfect for our needs. Our research of the town's statistics tells us it's ripe for some sort of industry. I've also met briefly with the mayor. He was a little vague, but he seemed like someone who would be willing to help when the time came. What's your opinion of him?"

"Jerry Ornett is a nice man."

Stratford nodded, satisfied. "Tell me a little more about the town and its people."

Martin shrugged, honestly bewildered. "I don't know what I can tell you. We're just an ordinary, small southern town. I—" He turned his head and narrowed his eyes against the gathering dusk. "That's funny. That sounds like a horse. Who would be riding out here at this time of night?"

Up in the hayloft, Rhiannon also gazed toward

the sound of the horse and saw a horse and rider emerge from the woods. Even in the fading light it was clear that the rider was dressed in Union blue and that his complexion appeared *very* pale. Amazed and delighted, she watched.

Martin's hands flew to his face. "Oh, my God, it's *him*."

"Him?" Stratford asked, then looked at the thunderstruck expression of the man beside him. "What's the matter?"

"John Miller. It's John Miller. I can't believe it. It's him! But what's he doing out here? He's not supposed to be here. And he's really late."

"Danger! Danger!" the rider yelled as he and the horse crossed the field. "The town is in danger! Save yourselves!"

"Oh, Lord," Martin said, grabbing Stratford's arm. "It's an omen. I told Arthur we shouldn't do it. Oh, my word, I wonder if John Miller's dangerous. He might try to kill you. Oh, Lord, he might try to kill me. I was helping you. Well, actually I was helping myself. That's even worse, isn't it?"

Stratford pried Martin's hand off his arm. "Get hold of yourself, man. What are you talking about? Who is John Miller?"

Martin's eyes were wild as he turned to Stratford. "Can't you see? He's a ghost. We've got to get out of here."

"Hold it right there. You're telling me that rider is a dead man? Come on, Martin. What kind of joke are you playing here?"

"The town is in danger!" the rider yelled, circling closer. "Save yourselves!"

Martin grabbed hold of Stratford's arms again, as much to keep himself from shaking as to make a point. "I don't have time to explain right now, but trust me. That man on that horse died over a hundred years ago, but he's very real. He's Hilary's ghost."

Stratford studied the overwrought man before him. "You really believe this, don't you?"

"Of course I do! Everyone does!"

"Are you saying the whole town believes in this ghost?"

"*Yes.* We always look for him at Halloween, but this year he was late. And now he's here, and he's upset. This is the first time he's ever ridden outside of town. Lord, this is really going to put the icing on the cake. Now the town will know for sure that it's wrong to let Collin come in here. John Miller saved us once before, and he's doing it again."

"Danger! Danger!" the rider shouted.

"This is ridiculous," Stratford muttered. "I've heard of people believing a house is haunted, but never a whole damn town."

"Don't you see? John Miller's upset because Collin Chemicals wants to come into Hilary. We've got to get out of here."

"All right," Stratford said, throwing a final disgruntled glance at the rider. "We'll leave, but Arthur and I are going to have a talk when I return to work tomorrow. He didn't tell me the town was crazy."

Behind them, the rider disappeared into the woods.

Up in the loft, Rhiannon laughed with joy.

Rhiannon launched herself into Noah's arms the minute he walked into her apartment later that evening. "Where have you been? I've been waiting and waiting."

He grinned down at her. Her golden hair looked as if she'd been out racing among the stars, and her scent enticed him to breathe her in. Best of all, her beautiful blue eyes were sparkling with happiness. "I'm sorry. I had a few things to do. Tell me, did you approve of my performance?"

"Approve? I loved it. I've got to know everything."

He laughed. "First, let's go sit down while I still can. I learned to ride at those summer camps my parents sent me to, but that was a long time ago. Tomorrow my muscles are going to be reminding me that I haven't been on a horse for years."

He sank onto the couch and drew her down beside him. Taking a moment to gaze around the room, he noted the fire crackling in the fireplace, Merlin in his position atop the armoire, Gray-malkin out in the flower box, surveying his kingdom. Everything was in its proper place, Noah thought with satisfaction.

"Start from the first. Where did you get the horse?"

"I borrowed him from a farmer Esme and Lavinia know. That's where I've been all this time. I had to return him, and then I had to scrub the makeup off and change."

"And where did you get the uniform? I don't carry Union uniforms in my shop."

"Esme and Lavinia whipped it up on their old treadle sewing machine this afternoon. They also made my face up. How did I look?"

"Very dead."

"Then I got the effect I was going after. How did Martin and Stratford react?"

"Martin completely went to pieces."

Noah nodded with satisfaction. "I figured his reaction would be more effective if he didn't know what I was up to. What about Stratford?"

"He's convinced that everyone in town should be committed."

"Good. And if, after a night's sleep, he wakes up in the morning wondering whether or not he might have jumped the gun in coming to that conclusion, he'll see all of Hilary in their Halloween finery. Only there'll be no explanation because it won't be Halloween."

Rhiannon laughed softly. "Oh, Noah, I can't tell you how happy it made me to see you out there in that field playing like you were John Miller. It was so out of character for you to do something like that."

He cupped his hand along her jaw and lightly

caressed her cheek with his thumb. "I wanted very much to help the town."

"You did. And you also helped me. You gave me answers that have been right there in front of me all along. Noah, I love you."

His hand stilled on her face. "You love me? Just like that?"

"In a way, yes. In another way, no. It seems as if that particular realization has been a long time coming, but then suddenly you rode out of the woods, and I knew. You see, I'd been bothered by the fact that you didn't belong in Hilary, and what's more, you didn't want to belong."

"I fell in love with you. I didn't have a choice but to fall in love with the town that's so important to you. Besides," he said with a wry grin, "I've come to the conclusion that Hilary's like a virus. It's contagious."

"No, don't gloss over it. For days, I saw you fighting against everything about this town, plus me. But, this afternoon, right before my eyes, you made yourself fit into Hilary and all of its absurdity because you loved me. And in doing that, you taught me more about love than you'll ever know. Hilary has been my stability for as long as I can remember. But now my stabilty is in our love. And I don't mind leaving."

He was having trouble keeping up with her. "Wait a minute. Are you saying you'll go back to New York with me?"

"Yes. Or anywhere else you want to go for that

matter. The life we'll make together will be worth it."

"And what about all those feelings you were so afraid of?"

Her eyes glinted with deep emotion. "Without those feelings, I might die. I've grown to *need* the way you make me feel."

With a groan he pulled her to him.

Moonlight spilled through the open window and fell in lace patterns across the bed and the two people who lay there talking quietly.

The iridescent ivory draperies stirred in the gentle breeze and Noah smoothed his hand over her bare shoulder and pressed a kiss to her hair. "There's one thing I really would like to ask you."

"You can ask me anything, Noah. You should know that."

"Okay, then, why do you wear black all the time?"

She turned her head toward him. "That's been bothering you?"

"Well . . . a little."

"It's quite simple. When I found Merlin, he was such a tiny frightened thing. That first week that I had him I concentrated so hard on making him live, that I didn't pay any attention to myself or what I was wearing. It was a coincidence that everything I wore that week was black. And of course, Graymalkin was always around, and he's black."

"Very."

"Well, Merlin grew stronger, time passed, and one day I put on something that was a bright color. When Merlin saw me he became so upset he started to tremble violently. That's when I realized he had bonded with me as I appear when I wear black clothes, and that unless I wore black I didn't look like his family."

"You wear black so as not to upset an owl?"

"Yes." She waited, and when he didn't say anything, she asked, "Well, is that an acceptable explanation?"

"It makes a certain type of sense, I suppose. But you know what? I don't care any more if you have a reasonable explanation for things or not."

"Really?"

"All that matters to me is that we're together and that you're happy." He came up on one elbow and looked down at her. "Rhiannon, I'd like to open a law office here. At first it would be a part time practice, but I have a very strong feeling it would evolve into full time eventually."

"Here? Won't you be bored?"

"Are you kidding? In Hilary? These people definitely require someone to look after them. Clifford needs all the help he can get. Besides, I can draw business from Richmond and other towns, and I'll still maintain my office in New York at least for a while. I'll have the best of both worlds. Most important, I'll have you."

She smiled. "Don't forget Graymalkin and Merlin."

"Trust me. Forgetting them would be impossible."

"Does your building allow pets?"

"If they don't, we'll move."

"The thing is, Graymalkin and Merlin are both used to their freedom. . . ."

"I know. Don't worry, we'll work something out for them. Maybe we'll leave them with Lavinia and Esme for a short time. Maybe a place in Connecticut is the answer. Maybe we'll just stay here forever."

"You're wonderful," she murmured.

He kissed her gently. "That's exactly how I feel about you."

They both heard the sound at the same time. A horse was walking down the main street of Hilary.

"It's John Miller," she said softly.

"How can you be so sure it's not just another teenager playing a prank?"

"Because there'd be no point. It's two days past Halloween. Besides, by now word has spread all over town that John Miller was seen out at Grandmother's. No, this is the real John Miller. Can't you tell?"

He listened. The horse walked slowly, hesitantly, as if its rider were searching for something or someone. "You're right," he whispered. "It's him."

"Aren't you going to get up and look?"

He shook his head. "No. I don't need proof. I need only you." He lightly fingered a long, curling blond strand of her hair. "But . . . well, there is one more thing I'd like you to tell me."

"What?"

He hesitated. "You really are a witch, aren't you?"

"Is that what you think?"

"Rhiannon, the power you have over me is undeniable and unprecedented. There's no doubt. You're a golden-haired, blue-eyed witch who cast a spell over me and stole my heart. Come on. Admit it."

A witchlike smile slowly spread across her face. "I love you," she whispered, and wrapped her arms around his neck and pulled him down to her.

The two lovers didn't notice when the horse's hooves grew distant. Nor did they notice the tinkling of the bell on Graymalkin's collar as, out in the window box, he turned his head and gazed after the horse and rider until they disappeared.

When he looked back, he was smiling.

And between his front paws, a blue sapphire cuff link glinted in the moonlight.

THE EDITOR'S CORNER

Get ready for a month chockfull of adventure and romance! In October our LOVESWEPT heroes are a bold and dashing group, and you'll envy the heroines who win their hearts.

Starting off the month, we have **HOT TOUCH**, LOVESWEPT #354. Deborah Smith brings to life a dreamy hero in rugged vet Paul Belue. When Caroline Fitzsimmons arrives at Paul's bayou mansion to train his pet wolf for a movie, she wishes she could tame the male of her species the way she works her magic with animals. The elegant and mysterious Caroline fascinates Paul and makes him burn for her caresses, and when he whispers "Chere" in his Cajun drawl, he melts her resistance. A unique and utterly sensual romance, **HOT TOUCH** sizzles!

Your enthusiastic response to Gail Douglas's work has thrilled us all and has set Gail's creative juices flowing. Her next offering is a quartet of books called *The Dreamweavers*. Hop onboard for your first romantic journey with Morgan Sinclair in LOVESWEPT #355, **SWASHBUCKLING LADY**. Morgan and her three sisters run The Dreamweavers, an innovative travel company. And you'll be along for the ride to places exotic as each falls in love with the man of her dreams.

When hero Cole Jameson spots alluring pirate queen Morgan, he thinks he's waltzed into an old Errol Flynn movie! But Morgan enjoys her role as Captain of a restored brigantine, and she plays it brilliantly for the tourists of Key West. In Morgan, Cole finds a woman who's totally guileless, totally without pretense—and he doesn't know how to react to her honesty, especially since he can't disclose his own reasons for being in Key West. Intrigued and infuriated by Cole's elusive nature, Morgan thinks she's sailing in unchar-

(continued)

tered waters. We guarantee you'll love these two charming characters—or we'll walk the plank!

One of our favorite writing teams, Adrienne Staff and Sally Goldenbaum return with **THE GREAT AMERICAN BACHELOR,** LOVESWEPT #356. Imagine you're on the worst blind date of your life . . . and then you're spirited away on a luxury yacht by a handsome hunk known in the tabloids as the Great American Bachelor! Cathy Stevenson is saved—literally—by Michael Winters when he pulls her from the ocean, and her nightmare turns into a romantic dream. Talk about envying a heroine! You'll definitely want to trade places with Cathy in this story of a modern day Robinson Crusoe and his lady love!

Peggy Webb will take you soaring beyond the stars with **HIGHER THAN EAGLES,** LOVESWEPT #357. From the first line you'll be drawn into this powerfully evocative romance.

A widow with a young son, Rachel Windham curses the fates who've brought the irresistible pilot Jacob Donovan back from his dangerous job of fighting oil rig fires. Jacob stalks her relentlessly, demanding she explain why she'd turned her back on him and fled into marriage to another man, and Rachel can't escape—not from the mistakes of the past, nor the yearning his mere presence stirs in her. Peggy does a superb job in leading Rachel and Jacob full circle through their hurts and disappointments to meet their destiny in each other's arms.

Next in our LOVESWEPT lineup is #358, **FAMILIAR WORDS** by Mary Kay McComas. Mary Kay creates vividly real characters in this sensitive love story between two single parents.

Beth Simms is mortified when her little boy, Scotty, calls ruggedly handsome Jack Reardan "daddy" during the middle of Sunday church services. She knows that every male Scotty sees is "daddy," but

(continued)

there's something different about this man whose wicked teasing makes her blush. Jack bulldozes Beth's defenses and forges a path straight to her heart. You won't want to miss this lively tale, it's peppered with humor and emotion as only Mary Kay can mix them!

Barbara Boswell finishes this dazzling month with **ONE STEP FROM PARADISE,** LOVESWEPT #359. Police officer Lianna Novak is furious when she's transferred to Burglary, but desire overwhelms her fury when she meets Detective Michael Kirvaly. Urged on by wild, dangerous feelings for Michael, Lianna risks everything by falling in love with her new partner. Michael's undeniable attraction to Lianna isn't standard operating procedure, but the minute the sultry firecracker with the sparkling eyes approached his desk, he knew he'd never let her go—even if he had to handcuff her to him and throw away the key. Barbara will really capture your heart with this delightful romance.

We're excited and curious to know what you think of our new look, so do write and tell us. We hope you enjoy it!

Best wishes from the entire LOVESWEPT staff,
Sincerely,

Carolyn Nichols

Carolyn Nichols
Editor
LOVESWEPT
Bantam Books
666 Fifth Avenue
New York, NY 10103

60 Minutes to a Better, More Beautiful You!

Now it's easier than ever to awaken your sensuality, stay slim forever—even make yourself irresistible. With Bantam's bestselling subliminal audio tapes, you're only 60 minutes away from a better, more beautiful you!

__ 45004-2	**Slim Forever**	$8.95
__ 45112-X	**Awaken Your Sensuality**	$7.95
__ 45081-6	**You're Irresistible**	$7.95
__ 45035-2	**Stop Smoking Forever**	$8.95
__ 45130-8	**Develop Your Intuition**	$7.95
__ 45022-0	**Positively Change Your Life**	$8.95
__ 45154-5	**Get What You Want**	$7.95
__ 45041-7	**Stress Free Forever**	$7.95
__ 45106-5	**Get a Good Night's Sleep**	$7.95
__ 45094-8	**Improve Your Concentration**	$7.95
__ 45172-3	**Develop A Perfect Memory**	$8.95